GABRIEL'S DREAMS

Martyn Croft

ISBN: 978-0-9559872-8-1

© Martyn Croft 2009

All Rights Reserved

This book is copyright. Subject to statutory exception and to provisions of relevant collective licensing agreements, no part of this publication may be reproduced, stored in a retrieval system, or transmitted in any form or by any means, without the prior written permission of the author.

In this work of fiction, the characters, places and events are either the product of the author's imagination or they are used entirely fictitiously. Any resemblance to actual persons, living or dead, is purely coincidental.

Cover Image by Digital Vision / Getty Images

For Susan, Hayley & Shell

'For there is no friend like a sister
In calm or stormy weather'
(Christina Rossetti 1830-1894)

CONTENTS

1.	A New Addition	7
2.	Dreams Future, Dreams Past	18
3.	A Winning Hand	33
4.	The Visit	45
5.	Escape	57
6.	Maggie May	69
7.	Dreams and Schemes	75
8.	A Stranger in the Crowd	89
9.	Through the Portal	95
10.	Tantrums	107
11.	The Mornings After	121
12.	Maggie's Secret Friend	130
13.	A Bloody Nose and a Strange Young Man	143
14.	Tests	153
15.	A Waking Nightmare	164
16.	Two Scans	173
17.	The Black-Haired Gypsy Boy	181
18.	A Walk in the Woods	185

1
A New Addition

It had been a long and, at times, an arduous wait, but the day had finally arrived when Naomi would give birth. Tuesday, June the 2nd, 1896 dawned warm and sunny in the fishing village of Fenton on the East Anglian coast. The would-be parents, Gabriel and Naomi Thomas, had had and eventful year since getting married the previous April. Apart from nearly losing his life in a storm at sea while fishing with his father, Joshua, Gabriel had experienced a series of unusually severe nightmares that had culminated in a few months bed-ridden in a catatonic state which no one – not even Dr Entwhistle – could explain. Other than a family history that contained one or two examples of extreme mental problems – Gabriel's elder sister, Mary, was a permanent resident in the nearby Canford Asylum – the coma-like state that Naomi's husband suffered went as quickly as it had come. It would be a continuing worry to Naomi and other members of Gabriel's immediate family that the family 'curse' – as Gabriel's mother was prone to call it – would return to haunt her and her son and heirs.

Naomi's labour was short, starting conveniently a couple of hours after sunrise and finishing with the birth of a baby boy at just after eleven that morning. Dr Winstanley Entwhistle, together with Nurse Ellen, attended to make sure everything went smoothly. The good doctor had kept a weather eye on Naomi and her husband ever since Gabriel's unfortunate 'illness' which had lasted from just before the previous Christmas till early April. It had taken all of the intervening months to restore Gabriel to full health, if not full fitness or weight and Dr Entwhistle knew more than most that relapses of his strange mental complaint could still suddenly occur, often sparked off by other unrelated events – whether traumatic or not. The birth of Gabriel's first child might be one such emotional event that could provide the catalyst – and that was reason enough for Dr Entwhistle's on-going concern.

It wasn't until half an hour after the birth that the anxious father was allowed into the bedroom where the significant event had taken place. He almost burst into tears when his wife immediately announced,

"You have a son, Gabriel."

"Thank the Lord, dear wife. We are blessed."

"Yes, and he has your black hair. Come, see."

Gabriel moved nervously towards the bed where the new-born baby lay in Naomi's arms. His wife smiled proudly and said,

"Come, Gabriel, hold him."

Gabriel sat on the bed beside his wife and took his son in his muscular arms for the very first time. He had already heard his son cry, seconds after the birth but that crescendo was to be nothing when compared to the noise that then emanated from his offspring's mouth. Naomi immediately reached for her baby to comfort him.

"Oh, Gabriel, you have a lot to learn about holding your son – he is quite upset. There, there my little one – your father has scared you."

Nurse Ellen came to Naomi's aid.

"He has powerful lungs, that one, Naomi, to be sure. I never heard the like before."

The baby's crying had suddenly brought the doctor and Naomi's mother, Mary Eliott, running into the bedroom from the kitchen where they had been tidying up after the birth.

"Whatever is the matter?" asked Naomi's mother, as soon as she entered the room. "Is my grandson alright, Ellen?"

"Oh, yes, Mrs Eliott – babies only want their mothers immediately after entry into this world. Gabriel here will be able to hold him in a few days without such commotion."

Nurse Ellen paused while she made mother and baby more comfortable and then continued,

"Naomi needs to rest now. I will stay with her while she sleeps and baby rests in his crib. You and your mother-in-law must leave now, Gabriel. Have you thought of a name for your son?"

Gabriel looked at Naomi for support, but her eyes looked heavy after her ordeal and she gave an exhausted smile. Gabriel answered for both of them.

"We have two or three, Ellen, but we haven't finally decided yet. It was going to be easy if it had been a girl, for we would have called her Mary after Naomi's mother and my …"

"Your?"

"His sister," said Naomi's mother. "I'm surprised you had to ask, Ellen."

The nurse looked slightly embarrassed at Mary Eliott having to remind her of Gabriel's tragic sister in the asylum.

"Oh, of course – how stupid of me to forget."

"Come, let us leave Ellen with Naomi and the baby," said Dr Entwhistle.

Gabriel seemed reluctant to leave his wife and their newly-born son – he appeared to want to prove to Naomi and himself that he could be a good father and that his son wouldn't cry again when he held him. However, his mother-in-law and Dr Entwhistle soon ushered him firmly out of the bedroom, giving him just enough time to kiss his wife and son, the latter act again causing the baby to exercise his lungs in protest.

"Go now, Gabriel," said Naomi. "You are scaring our son," and then, seeing her husband's frustration, she continued, "He will take to you in a few days, just like Ellen said."

But Gabriel would be hurt several more times over the ensuing weeks as his son would continue to object whenever he attempted to hold him in his arms.

The choice of a name for the happy couple's son proved to be a cause for some debate, if not argument, between Naomi and Gabriel and matters came to a head at teatime on the Sunday following the birth. Naomi's parents, Mary and Richard Eliott, had been invited for the afternoon, it being the most convenient time for her father to be present. As Mayor of Fenton, he had little free time to spend with his family, particularly with the Queen's diamond jubilee imminent the following year and all the civic preparations that that would entail. Naomi and Gabriel had shelved any discussion about their boy's name for over twenty-four hours, each hoping that they would gain support for their choice from their own families. Gabriel soon found himself pinned in a corner when Naomi's mother inevitably opened the debate.

"Well, have you come up with a name yet for our grandson?"

Gabriel looked at his wife, not daring to put his choice first.

"You know what I want to call him, Mother," said Naomi.

Mary Eliott looked a little nonplussed.

"Do I?"

"Yes – I thought you said you liked my idea of calling him after my father's middle name."

"What – Peter?" queried her father.

"Yes," said Naomi, briefly.

"Oh," said Naomi's mother. "I know I said I liked the idea but I also said it was up to you and Gabriel, dear. What does Gabriel think?"

Gabriel sighed – their argument was going to be aired in front of his wife's parents and he didn't like it. Richard Eliott came to his rescue.

"If he is to be named after a close family member then I think the name should come from Gabriel's side. After all, the child is a boy. If it had been a girl, then naming her after your mother would be sensible, Naomi. What is your suggestion, Gabriel?"

"Well, I would like to have my father's name, Joshua, but I had rather hoped to have a non-family name as well. I've always liked Edward – I don't know why; maybe I dreamt it or something. It just seems appropriate."

"Surely there is a compromise," replied Naomi's father.

Richard Eliott was used to tricky situations that required negotiation, given his role in life and, after a pause, he looked at Gabriel and his daughter and said,

"Why not name your son Edward Joshua Peter Thomas?"

Then Naomi's father seemed to remember something else.

"You know, Naomi, your great-grandfather's name was Edward, don't you?"

Naomi looked surprised.

"No – really?"

"Oh yes, my dear daughter. I think your choice is settled."

Gabriel looked elated; Naomi also seemed pleased.

"So," she said. "Our son will be named Edward Joshua Thomas, Gabriel. It has a nice ring to it."

"Thank you, Naomi," said Gabriel. "We will have a son who is a king, a leader and a disciple. How can he go wrong?"

Naomi's father grinned – his ruse had worked. Had he still been alive, his grandfather, Edwin Eliott, might also have smiled at his grandson's little white lie. Mary Eliott would scold her husband later for his blurring of reality.

Edward Thomas proceeded to give Gabriel cause to doubt his ability as a father for most of the summer of '96, almost leading him to question whether he would ever be able to hold and cuddle his son without him dissolving into floods of tears. Gradually, during the autumn, however, a tolerance grew between son and father and though Edward never actually produced a smile for Gabriel – preferring to stare at him with a wide-eyed glare instead – the crying did eventually stop in time for his first Christmas.

The day itself was to be a quiet family affair in the more affluent surroundings of *Fair View,* the cliff-top residence of Mayor Richard Eliott and his wife. Though only a hundred yards further along the cliff track from the young couple's own modest dwelling, it would be a somewhat experimental trek for Naomi and Gabriel to take their six-month-old baby through the thick snow that had lain in Fenton for a week or more that winter. While most of the poorer residents of Fenton used converted handcarts for the purpose, the town's mayor had provided his daughter and son-in-law with the latest design in pram. Naomi had spent many a happy afternoon proudly wheeling Edward through the streets of the small seaside village, even on occasions taking him at sundown to the South Quay to 'watch' his father and grandfather bring their fishing smack in from a day's fishing for mackerel, to be sold in Hamsden market the following day. With the newly-opened Beach Station operational, it had made the selling of their daily catch at the market, fourteen miles away, a much easier exercise. Though the pram was a godsend for Naomi on such trips, it would, however, be of no use that cold and snowy Christmas morning and Gabriel and Naomi would have to make the short walk to *Fair View* without any man-made device for transporting their baby son.

With several gifts to carry, as well as all the necessary clothing and equipment for young Edward, both parents had their arms full as they set off just after eleven on a crisp and frosty Christmas morning. The snow still lay several inches deep and they had to exercise great care when negotiating the unfenced track-cum-path which meandered uncomfortably close to the cliff edge in places. Naomi led the way, with Edward held close to her bosom and buried under layers of blankets, while Gabriel walked diligently behind, carrying all the non-animate gifts and paraphernalia.

They had trudged about half the distance when, for no apparent reason, Edward seemed to get excited and began wriggling in his mother's arms, causing Naomi to readjust his position against her right shoulder. From his new vantage point, looking back over Naomi's shoulder, he suddenly let out a scream when he spotted his father swathed in his long black coat and balaclava-like hat.

"Oh, Edward," said Naomi. "It is only your father, my little one."

Then it happened. In struggling to bury himself in his mother's bosom, Edward caused Naomi to turn abruptly and she lost her footing on a particularly slippery part of the track. She screamed,

"Gabriel! Help me – I'm falling!"

Gabriel was quick. He dispensed with all of his packages and dived forward in one movement. Naomi was already sliding and tumbling towards the cliff edge but her maternal instincts took over as she tossed her baby away from her body for Gabriel to catch. Edward landed gently in his father's outstretched arms as they both slithered along the soft snow.

Gabriel would never forget the look in his son's eyes as their faces were thrust together. It wasn't a frightened look, or, indeed, one of natural relief, but more a curious arrogant grin that lasted only for a spilt second before Edward dissolved into the expected screams. Those screams could not drown out those of Gabriel's wife as she had continued her slow, but uncontrollable slide towards the cliff edge.

"Help! Oh, please God, save me!"

Again, Gabriel was quick and he made a lunge for one of his wife's trailing legs with his free hand. It closed powerfully round Naomi's black leather boot, and, with almost superhuman effort, he halted her slide to inevitable disaster. Clutching his son tightly to his chest, he managed to haul Naomi away from the imminent danger and together they rolled over the snow to safety. By this time – and the whole event had taken a mere few seconds – Edward had become quiet again as his father passed him carefully over to his mother where he clung to her with face buried in her winter coat. As the young couple lay in the snow, both emotionally and physically exhausted, Gabriel could not fail but notice the same odd look which his son had given him seconds earlier, as he raised himself on unsteady arms and turned his head to stare at his father. It registered in Gabriel's mind as: '*So you think that makes you a good father, eh?*' That look would haunt Gabriel for some time – it had been one of disdain, rather than of thanks for or acknowledgement of a heroic deed.

Collecting the gifts – some of whose paper wrapping was damaged and sodden – would prove something of a problem for Gabriel after he and Naomi had eventually brushed the snow away from their clothes and reclaimed what they could of their possessions. The heaviest, a large tin of tobacco for Naomi's father, had slithered its way to the bottom of the cliff, whilst a couple of lighter ones had slid half-way down the sloping cliff sides and were partially buried in the thick snow. With the immediate priority to get his wife and baby son to the safety of *Fair View* – and with the inevitable fuss that ensued when Naomi and Gabriel reported their mishap – it was nearly forty minutes before Gabriel was able to go back and investigate the whereabouts of the three missing gifts. Fortunately, when he did, he was able to locate all of them by starting at the foot of the cliff and working his way slowly up the snow-covered surface, his progress made all the easier by deep footholds in the snow.

By the time he returned to *Fair View*, Naomi had recovered from her ordeal and was warming herself by the big open log fire in her parent's sitting room. Apart from a slightly bruised elbow, she was none the worse for her fortunate escape. Gabriel was naturally very attentive when he joined her for a few minutes quiet reflection, as Naomi's parents were putting the final touches to the Christmas dinner. Baby Edward seemed content as he lay asleep in the wooden crib that Naomi herself had once occupied more than twenty-three years previously. As soon as he entered the cosy parlour, Gabriel knelt down beside his wife and took her still-trembling hands in his.

"God has protected our family today, my love."

"Indeed, Gabriel – when I think what might have happened, I go cold at the thought."

Gabriel glanced nervously at the crib beside his wife's fireside chair.

"And how is my son?"

"He seems fine. I have fed him while you were gone and he took it well. He has been drifting in and out of sleep. See – he is trying to look at you, dearest."

Gabriel stood up and peered anxiously into the crib. To his great relief, the look had gone, whether imagined or not, and Edward grinned naturally at his father. And when Gabriel knelt down again to kiss his son's cheek, there were no histrionics; no tears and just a few gurgling noises of contentment, which prompted his mother to remark,

"He is thanking you, Gabriel, for saving him. He does love you and I think he is getting used to you now. Maybe today has been the start of a bond between you both."

"I hope so, Naomi, dear. I still have much to learn as a father. I cannot wait for the day when he is old enough to join me and his grandfather as a fisherman on the *Richard Goodman*."

"Oh, Gabriel, let us wait and see what our son will become – he may be clever enough to follow his other grandfather into his profession at the bank."

"What's that you say, Naomi, about the bank?"

Richard Eliott had suddenly joined them, having obviously been ushered out of the kitchen where he had, no doubt, been offering his usual mayoral advice in the last minute preparations for their Christmas feast.

"Oh, nothing, Father – Gabriel was just saying how he hoped Edward would become a fisherman like him. I was merely remarking that no one could possibly predict what he would eventually do for a living, that's all."

"I see, Naomi," replied her father. "And you think he might join my profession, eh?"

"Maybe."

"Well, I think that will be up to Edward himself to decide, don't you?"

Gabriel noticed that his father-in-law glanced in his direction as he posed his slightly rhetorical question. There was an unmistakable admonition in the statement about how his son's future should be handled and a comment on his own fatherly role in bringing him up. Naomi replied,

"Of course, Father. He may become anything – a soldier; a man of the cloth; a teacher or, indeed, a financier or a fisherman. God will decide, and as long as he grows up healthily and happy, we can ask for nothing more."

As if to give its own emphasis to Naomi's hopes for her son's future, a gong sounded from the hall, to be followed by her mother calling out,

"Dinner awaits you!"

2
Dreams Future, Dreams Past

The Christmas lunch at *Fair View* proved to be an extended affair, with both parents and grandparents using the occasion of the Lord's birthday to celebrate their own addition to the family. It was also to be the first Christmas Day when Gabriel would not be able to see his own parents. Annie and Joshua had taken the opportunity to visit Gabriel's aging maternal grandparents in Hamsden, with whom they were staying for a few days. It was likely that their stay would be longer than their intended duration owing to the heavy snowfall of recent days. No coaches had plied the Fenton-Hamsden road since before Christmas Eve and the small neighbouring market town would remain inaccessible by road almost until New Year.

With Richard Eliott's home-made wine flowing freely that lunchtime, Gabriel's thoughts eventually turned to the remaining member of his family – his sister, Mary. Gabriel rarely spoke of his tragic sibling and it was only a chance remark from Naomi's mother about her daughter's intentions for the future expansion of her and Gabriel's family that opened up the discussion.

"I expect you would like a daughter, Naomi – a sister for Edward, eh?"

"Oh, Mother – there's time a-plenty for that. Edward is not a year-old till June. Besides, I think Gabriel may prefer another son. Two boys may be more fulfilling in the long run."

Naomi turned to her husband for confirmation of her opinion, but none was immediately forthcoming and there seemed to be an awkward silence in the air until Naomi's mother asked,

"What do you mean by 'fulfilling', love?"

"I don't know what I meant by it. Maybe I used the wrong word, Mother, but Gabriel knows what I mean."

Mary and Richard Eliott turned to look at Gabriel who had taken a long swig from his after-dinner brandy glass.

"Well – what *does* she mean, son-in-law?" queried Naomi's father.

Gabriel said nothing. Beads of perspiration exuded from his forehead and, without a word, he dropped his napkin on the table, stood up and walked quickly out of the room. Seconds later they heard the front door open and close loudly to be followed by another awkward silence in the Eliott's dining room. Mary Eliott looked bemused when her daughter didn't immediately get up and follow her husband to see what was wrong.

"Whatever is the matter with Gabriel, Naomi? Where has he gone? Shouldn't we …?"

"No, Mother – leave him be. He will come back in when he's ready."

"But it's freezing outside, dear, and the snow still lies thick on the ground. Is he sick?"

"No, not sick," replied Naomi. "Just …."

"Just what?" interjected her father.

"Just worried – that's all," replied his daughter, quietly.

Genuine concern was etched on Naomi's mother's face.

"Worried? What about, love?"

Richard Eliott smiled sympathetically and reached across the table to touch his daughter-in-law's hand. He had guessed what was troubling Gabriel.

"It's your mother's namesake, isn't it, Naomi – his sister?"

"Yes."

"But why?" said Naomi's mother. Her daughter smiled wistfully and replied,

"He's just afraid that whatever happened to Mary will be passed on down the female side of the family. He says his grandmother on Annie's side went a similar way."

"But Annie is fine. You couldn't find a more level-headed and sane woman. Gabriel is lucky to have such a fine mother."

"I know, Mother, but we didn't see what actually happened to Mary. Gabriel was only six when she was taken to the asylum and, anyway, aren't you forgetting something?"

"What?"

"Oh, come on, Mother – remember what happened to Gabriel almost exactly a year ago. To all intents and purpose, and certainly as far as Dr Entwhistle was concerned, Gabriel himself was classed as insane for over three months. No one knows what that illness and coma did to his mind. Just put yourself in his position. You don't realise how nervous he was even before Edward was born, in case we should be delivered of a monster of some kind. He feels incredibly lucky and blessed that his son is a normal healthy baby."

"Oh," said Naomi's mother. "I hadn't realised – I'm sorry, love."

"Don't be – just try and understand and appreciate how Gabriel feels about raising a family. For him, it's much, much more than the normal responsibility. I often find him studying Edward as though he is looking for any demons that may already be inside his tiny head. I still think that the reason Edward always used to cry when his father held him was precisely because he could sense Gabriel's wariness of him."

By this time, tears had begun to well up in Naomi's eyes and they flowed freely when she made her next remark.

"And, Mother – we may never have any more children."

Before anyone could say anything else, they heard the reassuring sound of the front door opening once more. Seconds later, Gabriel reappeared in the dining room. Though he looked somewhat sheepish after his sudden and unexplained exit, he could not fail to sense the warmth of feeling that there was for him. Without a word, both his in-laws stood up and placed one arm round each of his shoulders as they escorted him back to his chair. Seeing Naomi's tear-stained face, Gabriel said,

"I'm sorry. I didn't mean to upset anyone. I just needed …."

"You don't need to say anything, son," said Naomi's father. "We understand. The subject is closed. Let us enjoy the remainder of this day in peace and harmony and let us thank God for our beautiful grandson."

Though Gabriel smiled at his father-in-law's reference to Edward, he still felt embarrassed that some of his innermost thoughts and fears had obviously been the topic of conversation while he had stood, crying, in the front garden of *Fair View*.

By the time it came for Gabriel, Naomi and Edward to go home that evening, it was quite clear to Richard Eliott and his wife that their son-in-law was in no fit state to make even the short walk back to his own house. He had consumed several more brandies after his 'walk-a-bout' and was very unsteady on his feet as he made to get up from his chair to go home a little after seven o'clock. Despite his protestations, Gabriel had to agree that, after the morning's events, discretion would be the better part of valour and he slumped back down beside the roaring fire, with relief written all over his face.

"I suppose you're right, Richard. I feel a little heady."

"A little?" queried Naomi. "I'm surprised you were able to stand at all, my love."

"Of course you must all stay," said Naomi's mother. "It looks a wicked night out there – it is snowing hard again. I'll go and prepare your old room, Naomi. I think Gabriel would welcome a bed very quickly by the look of him. Edward can sleep in the crib beside you both when you retire, love."

Gabriel didn't need much more persuading to go upstairs to bed and within half an hour Naomi escorted him to her old bedroom at the front of *Fair View*, overlooking the cliff and the sea. As she pulled the drapes to, she stared for a moment at the scene outside. It had stopped snowing and a full moon lit the choppy sea, highlighting its black and oily surface. The wind was getting up, blowing the new-fallen snow into drifts on the road below. It would have been folly to have walked home with Edward that night, she observed. She turned back to her husband to say goodnight, but he was already fast asleep and snoring contentedly.

The sea was getting rougher, as the feeling of déjà vu came to Gabriel. What was happening? The boat he was on seemed familiar but it wasn't the *Richard Goodman*; it was older. And then it hit him – it was his father's old smack – the *Rosalind Ann*. This could not be real. That boat had been wrecked in a storm, nearly two years previously. What was he doing there? Suddenly, his father called to him,

"Fast as you can both, my boys!"

Gabriel looked at the stern of the boat. Amos was not at the tiller – it was swinging left and right. Where was old Amos? He always came with them on fishing trips, even when he'd had too much to drink the night before. Gabriel tried to call out, but no words came. He found himself diving for the vacant tiller.

"*It's alright, Father – I've got it*," said a childlike voice which sounded familiar and was coming from nearby. Gabriel looked to his right. There was no one there. He managed to mouth a single word.

"Edward?"

"*Yes, Father. Don't worry – I'm in control now.*"

Gabriel tried to shake his head, but he couldn't move a muscle – his body was rigid, but he seemed unafraid. He had a strange feeling of contentment as he watched his baby son – naked apart from a cotton nappy – floated across the rear deck where he seemed to hover over the swinging tiller. Immediately, the tiller stopped its frenzied movement and the Rosalind Ann seemed to steady herself momentarily. Edward then raised his small arm and waved to his father. The baby shouted over the noise of the storm,

"*Goodbye, Father – I'm going to the asylum now!*"

With that, Edward turned and floated over the stern of the boat and disappeared over the side into the raging sea. Gabriel's movement returned and he scrambled across the bucking deck. Using the tiller for support, he looked over the stern. His baby son was floating on the surface, his tiny arms outstretched to his father.

"*Help me!*"

And then Edward was gone, sinking below the waves – a strange smile on his face as he looked back at his father above him. Gabriel dived into the black and violent sea. He screamed,

"I'm coming, Edward! Don't drown!"

"*Shh, Gabriel – you've woken Edward. Oh, how he cries*! *He is bathed in sweat.*"

"He's drowning! He's drowning!"

"*Oh, wake up, Gabriel. He's not that wet, my love.*"

"What? Oh …."

"*You've been dreaming, Gabriel.*"

Gabriel shook his head for real this time and, rubbing his eyes, sat bolt upright in the bed.

"Oh, I'm sorry, Naomi."

"What were you dreaming about?" asked Naomi, anxiously.

"Oh, er – It has gone now, but …."

"Yes?"

"I think I was at sea on the boat and it was stormy and …."

"And?"

"And nothing."

"Well, it didn't seem like nothing to me," said Naomi. "It sounded like you thought Edward was drowning. Was he?"

"I don't know, dearest. It was like I was back on the Rosalind Ann when she beached in the storm two years ago, but I don't remember anything else."

"I hope you're not going to start having your bad dreams again. You know what happened last time, don't you?"

"Yes, I know, but it wasn't quite like that, I think. It was somehow different."

"But you said you couldn't remember anything."

"I can't – it's just a feeling, that's all."

By this time, Edward had stopped crying as Naomi nursed him against her chest. She placed him back in his crib and, within seconds, his eyes closed and he returned to sleep. Naomi turned to her husband and felt his forehead.

"Well, you and Edward are both wet with sweat, Gabriel. It must have been a powerful dream."

"Probably just the brandy, Naomi," said Gabriel.

"Brandy, indeed. No more of that for you, I'm afraid. Strong spirits do not agree with you."

"Yes, dearest."

Naomi put her arm round her husband's shoulders as memories of another night returned to haunt her.

"You don't have a headache, do you, Gabriel?"

"No – I feel fine. I'm just tired, that's all."

"Well, I hope you get some more sleep. There's a gale raging outside. Listen."

But Gabriel didn't listen as sleep had returned to him almost instantly. Naomi lay down beside him, but she would not sleep for some time that night, as she laid awake thinking and worrying that the bad dreams might have started to return for a second time.

Despite his wife's urgings for him to steer clear of strong drink, it was not to be long before Gabriel again felt the need to celebrate with a few tots of his other favourite tipple – whisky. New Years' Eve was always commemorated well in the Thomas household, it being Annie's birthday, and this year was extra special – she was going to be fifty. Gabriel and Naomi had been invited to join his parents while baby Edward would stay with his other grandparents at *Fair View*.

Annie and Joshua lived on the very southernmost edge of Fenton, almost opposite the newly opened Beach Station in a modest fisherman's cottage; at the other end of the housing scale by comparison with Naomi's parents' house. By the 31st of December, the weather had improved considerably, with little lying snow left to cause any problems for the half-mile walk along the cliffs to the path that led down below St Andrew's Church to the beachside road below. A similar distance along this road, aptly named Undercliff, led to number 7 South Beach Terrace. It would be only the second time since Edward's birth that Naomi and Gabriel would spend the evening away from their baby son and, while Gabriel seemed relaxed with the arrangement, Naomi seemed anxious as they set off from her parents' house soon after dusk, having just delivered Edward safely to *Fair View*. The evening was mild, with a touch of sea mist rolling in and hanging in the hollows below them as they walked along the cliff top. Naomi linked arms with her husband, both for support and out of affection.

"I do hope Edward doesn't cry when he is with Mother and Father," she said. "He did before when I was ill and you were away fishing, Gabriel."

"Don't worry, Naomi – he doesn't cry like he used to. I feel he has taken to me at last."

"Yes, but my father sometimes upsets him with his deep voice."

Gabriel put his arm round Naomi's shoulders and said,

"He'll be fine, dear – he has a mind of his own and he will cope with anyone now, I think."

"I hope so – he got so upset on Christmas Day. I honestly thought he was getting a fever – he was so wet."

Gabriel was silent for a few paces as he struggled to remember the dream that had caused him to disturb his wife and son, but nothing would come back to him. They had reached the path that sloped down to the beach below. Naomi brought Gabriel out of his quiet reflection.

"Now hold me tight. It may still be slippery from the snow. I don't want to fall again."

The path was now more muddy than icy and by the time they reached the foot of the cliff, their boots were almost ankle-deep in the sandy clay. Fortunately, the tide was in and they were able to paddle their boots clean. Ten minutes later and they were outside number 7 South Beach where, before entering, Naomi kissed her husband lightly on the cheek. The short stroll, unaccompanied by Edward, had been a timely reminder of walks taken in the past when romance, and not family matters, had been more of a priority in their lives.

Annie was waiting in the lobby that doubled as a hall when Gabriel and Naomi walked in and she had a strange but pleased look on her face. As her son bent down and gave his mother his usual kiss on her forehead – she was five foot to Gabriel's six – he could feel her body trembling with excitement. His father was standing behind his wife with an equally warm smile.

"Hello, Ma – you look unusually pleased to be fifty."

"I am, but I also have some other news, Gabriel. Come through into the parlour and get warm. Leave your coats on the stand."

A few minutes later, with Naomi, Gabriel and Joshua seated and Annie standing by the open fire, she made her announcement – words that Gabriel thought he'd never ever hear.

"Mary has been asking for you, Gabriel."

At first, Gabriel seemed not to have heard his mother and he looked slightly confused until Annie continued.

"She has spoken your name."

"She has said something, Mother? How do you know?"

"The warden sent his quarterly report to Dr Entwhistle as usual at this time of the month and he came to see me this morning with the news."

Gabriel still didn't seem able to take in what his mother was saying.

"And she asked specifically for me?"

"Well, Dr Entwhistle said she mentioned your name twice in the last week. You know she hasn't spoken for several years apart from her usual nonsensical sounds. Dr Entwhistle told me that the report says that it is the first time, almost since they took her away, that she has spoken any word that was remotely recognisable. And he also told me …."

Here Annie seemed on the point of breaking down into tears.

"What?" asked Naomi, now excited at her mother-in-law's news.

Annie gathered her thoughts and replied,

"Dr Entwhistle says that we can go and see her. I haven't seen her in more than five years, Gabriel, after that time when she …."

"I know, Ma, it was frightening and she might have hurt you badly. Are you sure that the doctors at the asylum think it will be safe?"

"Yes, the report says that she has been much quieter this autumn and has been much less of a handful. Will you come with me, Gabriel?"

Gabriel's father stood up and put his arm round his wife as she finally gave way to her emotions and wept uncontrollably.

"There, there, Ma – don't go upsetting yourself. You know what Dr Entwhistle said about not building your hopes up. Mary has an incurable illness and she can never ever be the same as she was when she was fourteen and they took her to the asylum. She is thirty-one now and God may take her before she is much older anyway. Dr Entwhistle said that in cases like Mary's the physical side deteriorates much more quickly than normal people, with her brain unable to function properly. It would be a blessing if the good Lord were to take her home."

"I know," sobbed Ma.

As Joshua led Annie to her chair, Gabriel asked,

"When did Dr Entwhistle say you could go? And, yes, of course I'll come. We all will, won't we, Father."

"Yes – we must all go. You will stay with Edward, won't you, Naomi?"

Naomi nodded her agreement and after Annie had dried her tears, she said,

"Dr Entwhistle said as soon as the weather gets better – maybe in the early spring."

"I'm sure that my father will arrange a carriage for you all to get to the asylum at Canford," said Naomi.

"No need," said Gabriel's father. "When we went last time we went by boat or, if we left it till after Easter, we could take the ferry across the River Wentham. It is only about a mile walk on the other side to the asylum. If you go by horse and carriage it's more than a twelve mile journey via the bridge further up the river."

"I'm not waiting till Easter," said Annie. "We'll go in the *Richard Goodman* as soon as the weather improves."

Joshua looked sternly at his wife.

"We'll go towards the end of February, love. Storms can spring up at a moment's notice in January and early February. It would be foolish to risk our lives. You know we rarely go out fishing this time of the year."

"We'll go on Mary's thirty-second birthday – February the 25th," replied Annie, with equal firmness.

"We'll see," said Joshua. "We will try to go as near as possible to that day – weather permitting."

A compromise had been reached and the arrangements would be put in place early in the new year when Dr Entwhistle would liaise with the asylum over the exact date. Nothing more was said on the matter as the four of them repaired to Annie and Joshua's humble kitchen for a fish supper, followed by Ma's speciality – Bakewell Pudding and custard.

Whether or not it was his mother's news about his sister, Mary, or a combination of the fiftieth birthday celebrations and the advent of the new year, Gabriel turned to the whisky bottle well before midnight. Naomi seemed reluctant to urge restraint, understanding that her husband needed to relax with the thought of a visit to his sister at the forefront of his mind. At one o'clock, however, Gabriel had reached a state where even his wife's tolerance was beginning to be severely tested. He had just returned from a call of nature when he only narrowly avoided tripping over his father's outstretched foot.

"Whoa, steady, son," said Joshua. "Sit down before you fall down."

"Gabriel!" said Naomi, loudly. "You have had enough now. It is well into the new year and I think you should make a resolution to be more abstemious."

Naomi's husband slurred his reply.

"Ye-es, my belov'd. I am …."

Gabriel's head dropped to his chest and his eyes closed in an alcoholic stupor.

"Right," said Joshua. "Let's get him to his bed, lass."

Annie said,

"No, husband, leave him be. You two will never get him up those narrow stairs. It's best that he sleeps where he is. I'll fetch some blankets and a bowl. He looks so peaceful and, besides, Naomi will get a better night's sleep without him tossing and turning beside her."

At first, Naomi insisted on staying with her husband until Annie and Joshua managed to persuade her to go upstairs. Gabriel's father assured her that he would check on his son after an hour or so; he was a light sleeper, he said. After she had got into bed, Naomi lay awake listening for her father-in-law's footsteps on the stairs, which would indicate that Joshua was fulfilling his promise. When she heard his footsteps for a second time as he returned upstairs, she finally drifted off to sleep in the knowledge that her husband seemed to be sleeping peacefully.

He was at sea again, but this time the weather was fair and the sun was burning down on his neck. He was on board the *Richard Goodman* with Joshua and Amos. They seemed becalmed with all their tackle deployed from the seaward side of the boat. Suddenly, a strange voice called to Gabriel from behind him as he tended to one of the nets. It was a girl's voice.

"Oh, my handsome brother, it is a beautiful day to be sure. How the sun glints off your back."

Though strange, the voice seemed familiar, a distant memory from Gabriel's past. He dared not turn round. Was it …? The he heard his father's voice.

"Come on, Mary, more baskets if you please, lass."

Gabriel forced himself to look behind him. His body seemed reluctant to move and he felt heavy and lethargic. After what seemed ages, he managed to turn. A girl of about sixteen stood before him – but it didn't look like his sister. This girl had long flowing blond hair; Mary's had been jet-black, like his, when he had last seen her as a fourteen-year-old girl. It couldn't be Mary – he would be only about eight if it was and he was in his twenties, wasn't he? What the girl said next also disturbed him.

"Edward – pass me those two empty baskets."

"I'm not Edward – he's at *Fair View*. I'm …."

"Come on, Ed, Father is waiting."

"I'm not Ed!" insisted Gabriel.

"For goodness sake, stop daydreaming and pass me the baskets!"

"But I'm not Ed!" shouted Gabriel. "I'm not Ed! I'm not Ed!" he screamed.

"Come on, Ed! Come on, Ed!"

"Come on, Gabriel, please wake up! Edward's not here, my love."

"Oh, what? Is that you, Ma..?"

"Gabriel, you've been dreaming again. I'm not Ma, it's your beloved wife."

Gabriel opened his eyes. Naomi bent down and threw her arms around her husband.

"Oh, thank God! What were you dreaming about? And why have you taken your shirt off? You'll catch your death."

Gabriel's eyes slowly adjusted to the dim light provided by the dying embers of the fire. His chest was bare from the waist up. He shivered with cold

"I was hot, Naomi. I must have been dreaming."

"Yes, and a very strange dream at that. Of course you're not Edward. You were screaming at the top of your voice. Who ever said you were?"

"I don't know. Did I mention anyone else?"

"Not that I heard, Gabriel. Can you remember anything?"

"No, I guess it was a whisky dream."

"Well, you've only yourself to blame for that. I didn't try to stop you this time as I knew you were thinking about your sister all evening."

"Ah yes, Mary," said Gabriel. "I think she may have been in my dream."

3
A Winning Hand

January proved to be a miserably cold and stormy month and the *Richard Goodman* never left its moorings at the South Quay. While Gabriel's father spent most of the days either mending the nets or at home with his wife, Annie, Gabriel often accompanied old Amos to the Mariner's Inn for extended lunches. Joshua seemed happy for his son to spend a few hours extra relaxation each day, and he was always diplomatic when Naomi occasionally asked him how Gabriel was occupying himself without any fishing to do. If she had logged the number of times that Gabriel's father had said that his son was repairing the fishing tackle, she might have begun to wonder whether her husband was repairing the nets and tackle of every fishing smack moored at both quays in Fenton harbour. She also never seemed to question why two or three days a week Gabriel appeared more than usually cheerful when he arrived home at dusk. Fortunately, for Gabriel, any traces of alcoholic odours on his breath were always heavily masked by the usual fishy smells that accompanied him for the remainder of the day after a morning on the *Richard Goodman*. For his part, Gabriel stuck solely to brown ale for his tipple and though he would often consume three large tankards, he did not descend into an early slumber each evening. He was attentive both to Naomi's and Edward's needs. He slept well at night and was spared any more puzzling and frightening visions.

By the end of the month, the weather began to improve somewhat and Joshua announced that they would set sail for the first fishing of the new year on Tuesday, February the 2nd. When Gabriel's father announced his decision at suppertime on the last Thursday in January, Annie seemed excited, with the prospect of the visit to her daughter in the Canford asylum now imminent. She had received a visit of her own that day from Dr Entwhistle and she was anxious to relay the information to both her husband and her son who had joined his parents for supper, while Naomi and her mother had taken Edward to see one of his aunties who lived close to Fenton's main station at the north end of the village. Joshua and Gabriel had barely managed to have a wash and were awaiting their supper when she said,

"Dr Entwhistle has had a letter from the warden at the asylum and the visit is all arranged. We can go on the 21st, a few days before Mary's birthday. It's a Sunday, so you won't have to miss a day's fishing, Joshua."

"Good, Ma," said Joshua. "We are going to try the waters off Canford next week anyway so we can check out the route and mooring on the other side of the river. What time did Dr Entwhistle say we could go?"

"Anytime after lunch. How long will it take?"

"I don't know exactly – it will depend on the tides, but I would have thought about an hour to Canford and then maybe twenty minutes to the asylum on foot. We would set off around eleven and we would probably have at least a couple of hours there before we would need to return to be home in daylight. I'll know more when we're back fishing next week."

"Good," said Annie. "And it will be nice to have some mackerel for our suppers again."

With that, she returned to frying her pan of sausages, contented that her dream was going to come true. Joshua then prodded his son's ribs and with a harsh look on his face, he whispered,

"Only a couple more days of playing cards in the Mariner's for you, my lad."

Gabriel's swarthy cheeks went a deeper shade of red as he realised that his father had been well aware of what he had got up to on his extended lunches. He said nothing but offered a guilty grin in return; it had been a somewhat lucrative pastime for the previous three or four weeks and he would miss his games of blackjack with Amos and his cronies, which they played in a quiet corner of the inn, out of sight of prying eyes – or so he had thought. With the weekend and Monday tied up with his family and preparations for the start of fishing on the Tuesday, Gabriel would have one last day to indulge in, what he considered to be, his innocent pastime. However, his father's words, though seemingly amiable, had possessed a sternness that was a salient reminder that his pastime was not, in any way, innocent and that he should take steps to desist in future. As he walked home to his house later that evening, he made a promise to himself that he would only play cards for money for one last time the following day. He knew it was wrong and if Naomi ever found out then …. He offered up a silent prayer that she would not.

That evening, Gabriel toyed with the idea of telling Naomi about his exploits at the Mariner's Inn but eventually thought better of it. He would exorcise his demons by having one last session with old Amos and his friends. Yes, he had been lucky with the fall of the cards, but the two or three pounds in winnings weighed heavily on his mind as well as in his purse. As he carried his son to bed that night, Gabriel made up his mind that all the ill-gotten gain would be given away to his fellow players in one last gesture of repentance the following day. It had only been a few short weeks since Edward had allowed his father to lay him down to rest at night and Gabriel didn't want to lose that privilege by flouting fate any longer. What God had given, God could also take away.

With Edward safely tucked up in his cot, Gabriel and Naomi returned to the discussion of the forthcoming visit to see Gabriel's sister. Apart from a brief mention by Gabriel, little had been said between them earlier that evening after Naomi and Edward had returned from their trip to see one of Mary Eliott's sisters. It was well after nine when they were able to sit down in their parlour and relax. Though Naomi was clearly pleased that the arrangements were finally in place for the visit to the asylum, she was, nonetheless, concerned about her husband's reaction to the reality that, after many years, he was going to see his sister again. They had hardly spoken about the impending visit since it had first been mooted by Annie on New Year's Eve. Both of them, for their own reasons, had always seemed reluctant to start a conversation about the matter that was drenched in emotion for Gabriel and his family. Even now, Naomi seemed to struggle with the right words to open the discussion, perhaps fearing that her husband would reach for the whisky bottle for comfort.

"Do you want me to come with you when you go to see Mary? My mother could have Edward for the day."

"No, I would rather go on my own with my parents. It is not a nice place to go to; there are things there that …."

"Are you sure?"

"Yes, I'm sure and besides, it may come to nothing. I'm not building my hopes up, you know."

"I know, my love. I just take comfort in the fact that you made a remarkable recovery from your illness last year."

"I wasn't mad like Mary, though."

Naomi said nothing. Gabriel still didn't know really what he had put his family through and what demonic state he had reached. As far as he was concerned he had been in a temporary coma brought about by a sudden fit; he remembered little if anything about what he had said or done in those few bedridden months.

"No, of course not," said Naomi, reassuringly.

"Anyway, we will see what we will see, and that's all there is to it," said Gabriel with some finality. Naomi could tell from her husband's serious expression that it was time to change the subject before the 'water of life' started to flow freely again.

"At least you can start fishing again, Gabriel. What have you to do tomorrow and Monday?"

"Not much – just unfurl and check the mainsail, but looking at the weather, we won't be able to do that until Monday."

"And tomorrow?"

Gabriel hesitated before replying.

"I don't know yet until I see my father and Amos in the morning. I expect we'll have lunch in the Mariner's like we always do on a Friday when we're not at sea, my dear – one last time before the season begins."

Though he knew his wife was aware of the longstanding custom, he hoped that she was also unaware that the once or twice-yearly indulgence had become a regular occurrence over the previous few weeks. Her brief smile of acknowledgement left Gabriel in two minds as to whether she knew more than he thought.

"Alright then, dear; just don't touch the whisky bottle."

"No, of course not."

With the fire beginning to die down, Naomi soon ushered her husband to bed, where, despite his sober state that night, Gabriel would soon be involved in another strange, but not entirely unpleasant, dream. And, for almost the first time, it was to be one not instigated by alcohol.

The Mariner's Inn was smoky and heavy with the smell of fishermen idling their day away before the season started in earnest the following week. Gabriel was desperately trying to recoup his losses and he was down to his last two pounds and a few shillings. It could be his last hand and Amos was the dealer; they had decided on five-card poker for their last gambling session.

"Right, me lads. Let's see the colour of tha' money."

Henry Smith, Bob Gaskell and Gabriel tossed their shillings into the centre of the table. Amos dealt the five cards. Gabriel took his hand close to his chest. He had two queens and three lower denomination cards. Henry changed three cards; Gabriel suspected he had a pair, too. Bob changed only one and Gabriel thought, flush or straight. He watched the faces, but read nothing from them. He took three cards and tried to show no emotion as he picked up another queen and two rags. Finally, Amos said,

"And the dealer takes none."

What was the old boy playing at? He couldn't have a straight, surely, could he?

"It's up to you, Henry, mate."

Henry Smith tossed a shilling onto the table and Bob Gaskell followed suit; Gabriel paused and studied his hand – it had to be the best one. He placed three shillings in the centre of the table and said,

"Your shilling and raise you two."

Amos smiled. He looked at his cards, weighing up the possibilities. He reached inside his pocket and produced several crumpled notes. He took one and laid it carefully on the table together with three silver coins.

"Your three bob and raise ya' ten."

Henry gave a gasp.

"Ten, Amos? What are you playing at?"

"Poker," replied Amos. "Now let's see if ya' brave enough, me lads."

Henry Smith wasn't, and he threw his cards into the middle to be quickly followed by Bob Gaskell. Three pairs of eyes looked at Gabriel. He pretended to study his cards, but he knew what he had to do. He had promised himself – all or nothing. He reached for his purse and nonchalantly withdrew a pound note, placing it carefully on top of Amos' ten-shilling note.

"A pound, Amos."

Amos was quick and three more notes appeared from his crumpled bundle.

"Your pound and raise you two. That'll cost ya' three to see me."

Gabriel hesitated; he had one pound and some coppers left. He had to fold. Then he looked at the old man's grinning face and he knew he was going to continue. Amos couldn't have a straight – he had to be bluffing. Then, before he sought help from his friends for a loan, he looked at Amos' cards. He couldn't believe his eyes; he was holding them the wrong way round for all to see! He glanced at Henry and Bob, but their expressions were passive; they hadn't noticed a thing. Gabriel looked again. Amos had five unrelated rags. It was like he was in a dream and he couldn't lose. He looked at Amos' cards again, but now all he could see were the backs of the cards. Bob broke his trance.

"You want me to lend you some money, Gabriel, lad?"

Without hesitation, Gabriel replied.

"Yes, Bob, how much can you spare?"

"Ten pounds do you?"

"Yes."

Bob Gaskell carefully counted out the ten pound notes and scribbled a note on a piece of paper that he'd pulled from his wallet.

"Here, sign this, Gabriel and I have two witnesses, lad."

Gabriel signed the note and took the money. He placed five pounds on the table.

"There's five, Amos. It'll cost you that to see me."

Amos was quick but he seemed agitated.

"There's another five, me lad. It'll cost *you* to see me. I ain't payin' nothing to see you."

Gabriel placed the remaining five notes onto the pile.

"Very well, let's see what you've got old timer."

Amos looked embarrassed and he threw his hand down in disgust without revealing its contents.

"It's yours, lad. Take it, take it!" he said loudly as he tipped up his chair and stormed out of the back room to go to the bar. Henry and Bob grinned at each other.

"About time too," said Henry Smith. "He's tried that trick once too often. Well done, Gabriel – you've made a tidy penny there, lad."

"Yes, Gabriel," said Bob. "And you can pay me back my ten pounds now, if you please."

Gabriel counted out the ten notes and handed them over, receiving the piece of paper in return. He had over ten pounds still left in his hand. It was nearly two week's wages. He would treat Naomi and Edward.

With their number one short, the card school quickly disbanded and Gabriel made his way out of the inn, but old Amos had to make one last jibe at his vanquisher as Gabriel emerged into the main saloon.

"I'll get you next time, me lad; just you wait and see."

"No, you won't, old man, 'cos I ain't going to play for money again."

"Oh, yes you will!" shouted Amos.

"Oh, no I won't!" shouted Gabriel equally loudly.

"Oh, yes you will!" repeated the old man.

"*Oh, no I won't!*"
"*Oh, wake up, Gabriel!*"
"*Oh, …!*"

Gabriel opened his eyes. Naomi was holding his head.

"What was that all about, my love?"

"I don't know – just another dream, I suppose."

"Well, you seemed to be quite angry with someone. Who was it?"

"Can't remember," he lied. "What did I say?"

"Not much – all I heard was something that sounded like '*no, I won't*' a couple of times, that's all. You said it quite loudly the second time."

"Did I say anything else?"

"No – nothing. Are you alright? You seem quite relaxed and happy this time."

"I am, Naomi. I don't think it was a bad dream, whatever it was."

As Gabriel lay back down beside his wife and sleep once again took over, he smiled to himself as he realised that, for the first time, he could recall virtually every piece of his dream, even down to the exact details of each of the two crucial hands of cards – his had been the two red queens, the queen of clubs, the seven of diamonds and the two of hearts. Though Amos had not revealed his hand, Gabriel had seen the four of hearts, the five and six of spades and the seven and jack of clubs. Though it was not a disagreeable feeling, what did it all mean? Could it be tomorrow that …?

Everything seemed the same when Gabriel sat down in the quiet corner of the Mariner's Inn on the Friday afternoon; the position of the players;

the atmosphere and even the initial conversation and badinage. It was too surreal for words and Gabriel was nervous. His anxiousness increased and he shuddered almost openly when, after half an hour, he picked up the hand he had been waiting for.

"You alright, lad?" asked Amos, after he had finished dealing. "You got a good 'un, then?"

"Er – no, old man," replied Gabriel, trying to hide his emotions. "A fly flew into my ear. Don't go building your hopes up. You'll be disappointed."

"We'll see," said Amos, staring knowingly at his own hand. "How many cards, Henry?"

Gabriel's dream was then played out, as Henry and Bob changed the predicted number of cards. However, Gabriel was too excited to notice when reality crucially took a slightly different path and Amos took one as well. The rest of the play didn't deviate from his dream, including the ten-pound loan from Bob and the final five-pound bet for Gabriel to see Amos' hand. Gabriel tried to recall his exact words as he laid the last note down. He was close.

"Alright, old timer, let's see what you've got."

Gabriel immediately knew something was wrong when Amos smiled triumphantly – no angry or frustrated face; no overturned chair, but just a few calm words as he laid his five cards on the table. He emphasized and repeated the rhyming sound of his hand.

"There you are, me lad – *straight to the eight – straight to the eight*, young Gabriel. Now, beat that if you can."

Henry Jones and Bob Gaskell winked at each other. The old boy had pulled off his usual coup. Gabriel looked at his three queens – they hadn't changed. He had lost well over ten pounds and he was in debt for the first time in his life. He mumbled his acceptance of defeat.

"Too good for me. You win, Amos."

Amos grinned with delight.

"That'll teach you to gamble beyond your means. Let us hope that your father or your wife don't find out, eh? I wonder what they'd say."

Gabriel took his humiliation with a wan smile. He had learnt his lesson. Old Amos stared into Gabriel's eyes and said,

"Don't worry, lad, they'll not hear of your loss from any of us."

Bob and Henry nodded in agreement.

"No more cards today," said Amos.

"No," said Bob Gaskell. "Poor old Gabriel owes me enough as it is."

Gabriel had taken his verbal punishment in silence, but eventually, in a quavering voice, he said,

"I'm not going to gamble ever again, my friends."

Amos continued to stare into Gabriel's eyes as if checking on the genuineness of his contrite statement.

"No, I don't think you ever will, lad," said Amos, sympathetically. "And I'm going to set the record straight for thee as well."

Amos paused while he counted out ten pounds. He handed the bundle of crumpled notes to Bob Gaskell.

"Here, Bob, Gabriel's debt is honoured. Now you've only lost your own money, lad, and not someone else's."

Gabriel made to protest, but he could tell from the old man's face that he would be offended if he did and Amos said,

"It has been worth ten pounds to see your new resolve."

Gabriel hung his head.

"Thank you, Amos."

Though it didn't feel the right thing to do, Gabriel said nothing more – he would make amends later by one means or another.

"Don't thank me, lad. I owe you much more than ten pounds. Remember, you saved my life when the *Rosalind Ann* was wrecked in the storm."

"You'll need change, then, Amos," said Bob, with a broad grin and, finally, the atmosphere was lightened.

As Gabriel made his way home that afternoon, he pondered the extraordinary events that day. Yes, he had learnt his lesson as far as gambling was concerned, but he had also learnt something else – dreams were not to be trusted – and that made him think back to the other times when fantasy and reality had seemed to cross swords in his dreams. Time would tell whether he would have to face that confrontation again in the future.

4
The Visit

The more Gabriel thought about it later that night, the more puzzled he became over the whole affair. Why had his dream lied to him when most of it had come true? It just didn't make sense, unless there was a predetermined purpose to it all. And when he saw Amos again on the Monday, another strange thought entered his head. Could dreams be used as a warning or, indeed, could another person influence those dreams to cause actions to take place in reality. Had Amos been aware of his part in his dream and, if he had, was he himself aware of it? What did it all mean for his other dreams – the ones in which his son and his sister had seemed to appear? Finally, who was the strange blond-haired girl that his father had called Mary, if it wasn't his sister?

Tuesday turned out to be a fine day with a gentle southerly breeze to aid the *Richard Goodman's* progress to the mouth of the Wentham. With the tide in by eleven o'clock, the prospects for fishing looked to be good as Joshua and Amos positioned the fishing smack about a hundred yards off the beach and moorings at Canford. He shouted to Gabriel, who was busy laying some nets,

"Forty minutes, son – it'll be less than an hour to Canford when we go to see Mary at the end of the month and much less if the wind is stronger."

"Not if we get a nor'easter," called Amos from his usual position at the tiller, where he was turning the boat to face the sea. "It'll take twice that if we get a bad 'un."

Then the old man winked at Gabriel, who had come to supervise the weighing of the anchor.

"We shouldn't *gamble* on the weather, should we, lad?"

Fortunately, Gabriel's father didn't seem to notice any added emphasis to the pertinent word and his son merely smiled nervously at the old man. How many times was he going to be reminded of his foolishness? He didn't want Amos to think he had some kind of hold over him. He had realised the error of his ways and he didn't need anyone constantly reminding him of it.

The mackerel seemed plentiful and by mid-afternoon, they had as much as they could carry to sell just on the South Quay without the need to take any to Hamsden market the following day.

"Home, boys," shouted Joshua. "That's enough for the first day back."

Gabriel and his father began reeling in the nets, and with a pale sun beginning to descend over Fenton, they set sail for the harbour. The return journey took nearly twice as long as the southerly breeze had strengthened into a force five or six. It was dusk by the time they moored against the South Quay, but discovered to their good fortune that they had been one of only two boats out that day. There was a sizeable crowd still waiting for their catch. With the price of mackerel at its highest, they found that they had nearly twice a normal day's takings. Gabriel announced the total after the count.

"Seventeen pounds, twelve shillings and fourpence, Father."

Though the actual total had been exactly a pound more, Joshua seemed ecstatic at the disclosure of their day's earnings.

"What a good day, boys! Here's the bag, Gabriel – fill it up. We'll take our shares later."

"I'm on my way," said Amos. "You can pay me later, Joshua – I'm off for me tea at the Mariner's."

Though it was going to be a case of 'robbing Peter to pay Paul', Gabriel had already planned what he was going to do next, and as the old man passed him on the quayside, he thrust a pound note into his hand, whispering,

"Here, Amos – I *am* going to pay you back all your winnings."

At first, Amos tried to decline the money, but seeing Joshua looking in their direction, he quickly pocketed the crumpled note and whispered back,

"Alright, lad, but there is no need."

"Yes, there is, if it'll keep you quiet over the matter," replied Gabriel, through clenched teeth.

By the time Sunday, February the 21st arrived, Gabriel had returned nearly half of Amos' winnings – the fishing had been exceptionally good with only one day where the weather had been too bad to set to sea. Gabriel parted company from Naomi and Edward just after nine on a mild and sunny morning with just enough of a breeze for a quick and safe sail to Canford seem eminently probable. Arriving at 7 South Beach Terrace and entering the kitchen, it was clear that Annie had been ready for some time and was anxious to get started on their journey.

"Come in, Gabriel – we are going to set off at ten. Your father says the tides will suit better then for our return."

"Yes, Ma, he may be right. It is a fine day as well."

Gabriel's mother had donned her Sunday best and was soon pacing up and down in her kitchen, seemingly at a loss as to know what to do next with herself in the haven that she usually commanded and dominated. Joshua was polishing his boots and smiled at his son.

"Your mother hardly slept a wink last night – she is so excited. Tell her to calm herself, Gabriel. We don't want her so agitated on board the *Richard Goodman*."

Gabriel put a loving arm round his mother and escorted her into the parlour, but within a couple of minutes she was up and exhorting Joshua to finish his preparations. Ten minutes later – at a quarter to ten – the three of them were on the cliff path and heading for the South Quay; neither man had been able to put Ma off any longer.

The crossing to Canford was both reasonably quick and smooth, though Annie's normal ruddy complexion did take on a shade a degree or two paler at times, but her constitution held firm and they found themselves gliding slowly towards the little wooden jetty within the hour. With the smack safely moored, they began to make their way along the narrow landing stage to the shingle beach. Joshua kept checking his silver pocket watch.

"We are going to be a might early. It is not yet eleven. You said they were not expecting us till after lunch, Ma."

"I have thought of that," replied Annie, as she linked arms with her husband. "There is something I want to do in the woods."

"Woods?" said Gabriel, as he turned round to query his mother's rather odd remark.

"Yes, you can see them to your right," said Ma. "And you will see – I want to get something for Mary."

"But, Mother, she cannot have anything, you know that," said her husband.

"Then I shall give them to the nurses. Now let us get going."

Annie urged Joshua forward and they were all soon at the top of the narrow beach and heading off the road towards a woodland path that wound into a small grove. Gabriel kept his own silent company a few yards to the rear. With the trees still bare of leaves, his mother's objective soon became apparent; the yellow carpets of wild narcissi were easily visible through the 'soldiers' of ash, oak and elder that seemed to guard and surround the several woodland glades. It would be a spring posy for his sister and a token of a world that Mary hadn't seen for years.

Though they had had plenty of time in hand when they entered the wood, their progress to the asylum was eventually slowed by a combination of two factors. First, Annie insisted on gathering as many daffodils as they could each carry and second, Joshua decided he thought he knew a short cut which avoided retracing their steps along the path they had come when they entered the wood. The going became difficult as the path narrowed and meandered downhill where, at its lowest point, they had to cross several yards of boggy ground. Despite the bareness of the trees, it had also become quite dark as they climbed laboriously up the other side, where they paused to recover their breath, causing Annie to observe,

"It is an enchanted wood. My grandmother used to tell me that it was haunted by elves and goblins, Gabriel."

"She did that to keep you from straying too far from the beaten track, I expect, Ma," said Joshua. "Anyway, when did you used to come here?"

"When I was a child and the ferry first started running in summer."

Gabriel looked around him. The place had an eerie feeling and suddenly, a flash of white light caught his eye to the right.

"What's that, Ma?"

"What? Where?"

"Over there, past that big oak tree," replied Gabriel, pointing at a spot about a hundred yards distant.

"I see nothing," said Ma.

Gabriel focussed his eyes again, but the light had gone.

"Just the sun reflecting of something," said Gabriel's dad, but none of them looked skywards to see that the sun had been obscured by clouds for several minutes.

They continued their progress out of the wood and were soon in sight of the grey-stoned and brooding edifice that was the notorious Canford Asylum, which suddenly loomed up at them from between the last few trees as they emerged into bright and cloud-free sunlight. Its high iron-barred fences made the asylum look more like a maximum security prison than a home for the mentally insane. Soon, after announcing their arrival at the small gatehouse, they entered the grounds proper, passing several staff and inmates, who were tending the immaculate lawns and, as yet, empty flower beds. It appeared that the asylum catered for all stages of mental degeneration and some of its 'patients' were obviously deemed fit and safe to help around the grounds.

"What lovely flowers, my dear."

Almost unnoticed on their walk to the main building, they had been approached by a middle-aged resident, holding a hoe and smiling sweetly at Ma.

"Can I have one?"

Annie looked nervous but selected a daffodil and gave it carefully to the woman. She took it and skipped lightly off to her flower bed where she proceeded to form a small hole into which she inserted the tall yellow flower. She stood back and admired her handiwork, but as the daffodil started to lean over and fall, she picked up her hoe and, in a sudden frenzy, squashed it into little pieces on the freshly turned earth. She continued to smash the hoe into the soil until a uniformed guardian ran over and escorted her, ranting and raving, back to the asylum. Her probation outside was over for a few more weeks.

"Now you see what you've done, Ma," said Joshua. "You just mustn't give the inmates anything, no matter how sane they may look on the outside, dear."

Annie did not reply as she thought about her own daughter. Perhaps bringing the daffodils had been a bad idea. She might have to give them to the nurses to spread round the asylum as they saw fit. Gabriel broke her train of thought.

"Come – let us go and see our Mary. It must be getting on."

"It is after one-thirty," said Joshua.

They had reached the main drive to the asylum and its blackened walls did nothing to lighten the mood of any visitors brave enough to come. The middle block had six storeys and was hemmed in, on either side, by two identical sprawling two-storied blocks. All the windows of the centre section were covered by iron grids whilst the lower blocks were bar-free; being the accommodation for the staff and low-risk inmates. On Annie's previous visit, her daughter had been on the ground floor of the high-risk section. Annie clung tightly to her husband as Gabriel led the way to the imposing oak-faced and studded twin front doors. He quickly reached for and yanked the iron ring that connected to a deep-sounding bell somewhere inside the asylum. Soon, footsteps could be heard echoing on the solid stone floors. The left-hand door opened slowly to reveal a short, plump matronly figure dressed in a dark blue uniform and small white cap. A small white cloth badge disclosed the middle-aged lady's identity as Senior Nurse Elaine Michelson.

"Good afternoon – you must be Mary's family. I'm Nurse Michelson. Please come in and follow me. I'm afraid the flowers will have to be left outside. One of the warders will collect them later. Thank you for bringing them."

The senior nurse seemed friendly enough but Gabriel could tell she was used to being obeyed instantly and without question, so he quickly took Annie's and Joshua's daffodils and carefully placed them with his own on the step outside the front door. Annie looked decidedly cross but made no protest as, with one hand, she handed the flowers to her son. He then ushered his parents forward into the large foyer. The nurse turned to Gabriel and said,

"Please wait here until Dr Cavendish comes. You may sit over there by the table."

The nurse had indicated a long high-backed and uncomfortable looking wooden monk's seat positioned against the right-hand wall. A long trestle table stood in front of the bench with a couple of newspapers on top for visitors to read. Joshua sat down and smiled at his wife.

"You will get us all into trouble, Ma, if that nurse catches you."

Gabriel's mother grinned as she suddenly produced a small bunch of daffodils that she had somehow concealed, either behind her back, or in the folds of her Sunday-best dress. She picked up one of the newspapers and carefully wrapped the flowers in it. She then placed the rolled paper between herself and Joshua as she sat down beside her husband. Gabriel walked away to study the various paintings on the oak-panelled walls. They all seemed to be of former wardens and doctors at the asylum, none of whom Gabriel recognised. He went a little cold as he stared at the gallery of stern faced custodians. Their sombre expressions said it all about the people that they had had to deal with over the years. He wondered what Dr Cavendish would be like. He was pleasantly surprised when he heard the doctor's voice from the spiral staircase at the end of the foyer.

"Ah – welcome, welcome. It is good of you all to come. You must be Mr and Mrs Thomas and this is …?"

"My son, Gabriel – Mary's younger brother," said Joshua, hastily. Dr Cavendish was a small man with receding brown hair, a goatee beard and pince-nez spectacles which seemed to float, almost unattached, to his nose. He strutted towards them, taking nearly twice as many steps as would seem necessary to cover the short distance from the foot of the stairs. He shook everyone's hand in turn, winking at Annie as he spotted the yellow daffodil heads peeping out from the rolled newspaper.

"Better not let Nurse Michelson see you with that, Mrs Thomas – but don't worry, I'll organise a vase when we get to Mary's room; she's on the third floor now. Come, follow me."

Dr Cavendish continued to chatter as they made their way up the two flights of stairs. Yes, Mary seemed a little more alert and no, she hadn't been violent for some months, he said. Her movement to the third floor, he continued, indicated that they now considered her to be of a lesser risk than the asylum's worst patients. After walking down a long corridor, lined on both sides by, what appeared to be, individual rooms, they finally found themselves standing outside Mary's. She'd always been afforded the privilege of isolation, partly at Annie and Joshua's request and partly for her own and the other patient's safety. This special dispensation hadn't been cheap for Gabriel's parents, but Naomi's father had recently been able to use his mayoral connections to keep the charges to a bare minimum. Having seen the frightening chaos of the communal wards when Mary had first arrived at the asylum, Annie had insisted, no matter what the cost, that her daughter would not suffer that kind ignominy.

Dr Cavendish produced a large set of keys from his jacket pocket and said,

"Please wait here while I check to see how Mary is."

Annie looked nervous as the doctor selected a key and turned it in the lock. He opened the door just enough for him to poke his head round the corner. No noise emanated from within. Soon, he opened the door wide and indicated that they should enter.

"She is quiet, as you will see," he said, as they filed past him. Annie gave a gasp when she saw her daughter for the first time in some years.

"Oh, how she has aged," she said.

Despite the brightness of the day, Mary's room was dimly lit with wooden latticework shutters pulled to in front of the iron grille. The room was sparsely furnished. Apart from the single metal bedstead, there was a wooden chair, a small dressing table and a tall chest of drawers. A jug and bowl stood on the dressing table – they seemed to be chained in some way to the walls of the room, or cell, as it might have been more accurately described. The floor and walls were devoid of anything else, whether movable or not. Mary sat on the floor in the centre of the room, her arms clasping her knees and her chin resting on them for support. She seemed to be rocking gently forwards and backwards. Her hair was short and swept back; it was prematurely grey for her age. She did not seem to notice when her visitors walked in. Annie sat on the bed while Gabriel and Joshua stood near the window. Dr Cavendish pulled the chair towards him so that he could sit facing Mary. He looked into her eyes and said,

"Mary, your mother and father are here."

No response.

"Mary, they have come a long way to see you."

Mary continued her gentle rocking, her eyes fixed on the floor in front of her. Dr Cavendish turned to Annie.

"Perhaps you would like to say something to her."

Annie began to stammer, her eyes heavy with tears.

"M-Mary, my love, I am here."

Still Mary showed no sign of acknowledgment.

Annie made as though she was going to touch her daughter's shoulders but the doctor quickly shook his head.

"Perhaps Gabriel would like to say something."

Gabriel came to stand in front of his sister. He knelt down and looked into her vacant eyes."

"Mary, it is I, Gabriel."

Still no response. Gabriel tried again but, again, without success, and though over the next half an hour or so, they all tried several times to elicit some kind of acknowledgement from Mary, it was clear that she was not going to respond that afternoon. Eventually, Dr Cavendish summed up what they were all feeling.

"I'm sorry, but I don't think Mary is receptive today. She is not going to say anything, I'm afraid. Though she has only mentioned Gabriel's name a couple of times, it is most unusual for her to remain sitting in such a way. I understand that she is often found pacing up and down her room and occasionally looking out through the window."

Annie got up from the bed and placed the rolled newspaper and flowers on her daughter's dressing table. Without saying a word she walked out of the room, quickly followed by Joshua and Dr Cavendish. Gabriel waited until they had left and then looked at his sister for one last time. Her eyes remained fixed on the floor. Gabriel turned away to leave the room.

"I will see you again very soon, Gabriel."

Gabriel froze mid-stride; one foot in the room; one foot in the corridor. He turned back to look at his sister. Surely he was dreaming; it made no sense. Was his mind playing tricks?

"What, Mary?"

Dr Cavendish seemed to be the only one that had heard Gabriel speak and as he came to lock the room, he said,

"Did you say something, Gabriel?"

Gabriel was still staring at his sister. Her position had not changed; her eyes were still vacant and her head was bowed to the floor. He had dreamt it. He turned back to the doctor, thoughts racing through his mind. What should he say? What could he say? Who would believe him? Only he had heard, or had he? He quickly recovered his composure.

"What? Oh, no, Dr Cavendish. I thought Mary said something but it was just wishful thinking, I suppose."

Dr Cavendish gave a knowing smile.

"Yes, it can happen, Gabriel, I'm afraid."

Later that day, as they made their way back to Fenton on the *Richard Goodman*, Gabriel had a chance to ponder what he thought he'd heard as he'd left his sister's room. Though he had passed it off to himself and the doctor as his mind playing tricks, he was, nevertheless, reasonably convinced that Mary *had* spoken the strange words. However, something about the way she had said the words had made him want to keep it from his parents and anyone else for that matter. Their tone had suggested that the strange remark had been for his ears and his ears only.

5
Escape

Though Annie had been very quiet on the walk back to the *Richard Goodman* and on the subsequent sail back to the South Quay, she began to open up when she and Joshua had finally settled down in their parlour later that evening. Gabriel had not stayed long after their return, anxious as he appeared to be to get back to Naomi and Edward. After her sudden departure from Mary's room, Joshua had decided to let his wife come to terms with the afternoon's disappointment in her own time. They had been sitting in silence for a while when Annie suddenly said,

"I was expecting too much, wasn't I?"

"Maybe," replied Joshua. "At least she wasn't like she was before."

Annie knew that her husband was referring to the violent nature of a previous visit and said,

"True – she was certainly quiet but I have never seen her in that position before. She almost looked like an …."

"Like an animal?"

"Yes."

Joshua tried not to give too much credence to his wife's remark and said,

"Gabriel took his visit well. I think he had been expecting much more even than you."

Annie smiled and said,

"Yes, he seemed quite cheerful on the way home. I know he was quiet, like me, but I saw him smiling to himself on several occasions. I wonder why, Joshua."

"He was just probably relieved that the visit was over. I know he had been worried about it over the past few weeks. Amos told me the other day that he had been spending more time than usual in the Mariner's Inn."

"Oh?" said Annie. "Did he say anything else?"

"No – just that he seemed preoccupied with himself – even refused to play cards with him and his friends. He said we should feel fortunate that our son doesn't gamble like some he could mention."

Unbeknown to Gabriel, Amos had obviously made a point of assuring Joshua of his son's self-restraint, and even though the old man had clearly bent the truth in the matter, Gabriel himself would have been genuinely grateful had he been aware of Amos' remarks about his indulgence in his previous vice.

For her part, Naomi was also somewhat surprised and relieved that evening when Gabriel arrived at *Fair View* to collect her and his son. On the walk back to their own house, she was anxious to learn of the afternoon's events.

"Well, how did it go, Gabriel? How was Mary? You said very little at my parent's house."

"Like I told your mother, there is little to tell. My sister said not a word and didn't look at any of us once," he lied. "She just sat on the floor and rocked back and forth on her haunches."

"But are you glad you went to see her?"

"Yes, of course, but I'm also glad it's over now."

"Will you go again?"

"I don't know, my love. Dr Cavendish said he would let us know if there were any significant changes in her condition. He seemed as disappointed as we were, I think."

Naomi stopped walking and turned to look into her husband's eyes in the moonlight.

"And you're sure there was nothing else?"

"Yes, I'm sure – why do you ask?"

"Oh, I don't know, Gabriel – you don't seem to be how I thought you would be."

"In what way?" asked Gabriel, nervously.

"You seem happier that I expected, given that Mary hadn't really changed for the better. Are you sure you're alright?"

"Yes, as I said, I'm just glad it's over."

"And you're not too upset?"

"No, what will be will be, and that's all there is to it," replied Gabriel with some finality. Naomi took the hint not to pry further and they completed their walk home in silence.

Though the subject would not be discussed by them again over the following week, it would not be very much longer until Dr Cavendish would make contact to report on Mary, but it would have nothing to do with a change in her condition, whether positive or negative.

The news came on the last Monday of March, though the details had been known at the asylum for a few days – they had tried to keep it as quiet as possible so as not to alarm anybody, especially the residents of the small neighbouring village of Canford. Dr Cavendish himself arrived unexpectedly at 7 South Beach Terrace just after lunch, conveyed in one of the asylum's horse and carriages driven by Harold Baines, the head coachman whose main responsibility was to transport the inmates to and from the asylum in the black, hearse-like brougham. Annie was understandably nervous and somewhat disconcerted when she heard the horse and carriage pull up outside the cottage. With Joshua at sea for the day, she was, at first, reluctant to open the door to the doctor, particularly after she had spotted the funereal nature of his transport. After several vain attempts at knocking on the door, Dr Cavendish called out as loudly as he dared, without causing any unnecessary commotion in the small close-knit community. He had already noticed one or two curtains being drawn back in some neighbouring cottages.

"Mrs Thomas – it's me, Dr Cavendish. I need to talk to you about Mary. Please don't be alarmed."

Annie looked again through her kitchen window and when she seemed satisfied that the doctor was unaccompanied and was on asylum business, she opened her front door. She could tell immediately from Charles Cavendish's face that he had come on a serious matter.

"Oh, Dr Cavendish," said Annie. "Whatever is the matter? Is it Mary? Has she spoken again?"

"No, Annie. May I come in for a few minutes, please?"

"Of course, Doctor."

Annie led the doctor through the kitchen, heavy with the aroma of baking bread, and through to the small parlour.

"I'm afraid I don't light a fire till later. Can I get you anything – a glass of elderberry cordial, perhaps, or something stronger for your journey?"

"No, thank you, Annie, this won't take long. I'm afraid I have some bad news."

Annie seemed ready for the worst, as she slumped into a fireside chair with both hands clasped to her face in shock.

"Oh, no!" she gasped. "Is she …?"

Dr Cavendish shook his head.

"No, not that we are aware, Annie, dear. I'm afraid she's gone missing."

"Missing – how?"

"Nobody is really sure. She was being taken to the infirmary for some treatment to her feet and, while there, she was left unattended for a few minutes. Unfortunately, it seems, her disappearance was not noticed until the orderly came back from attending to a more urgent case. Of course, we immediately raised the alarm and searched the grounds and later, the local woods as well, but to no avail."

"When was this?" asked Annie.

"Last Friday morning. We've only just made the local Canford constabulary aware. It took most of the weekend to search the buildings and grounds; it's such a large area. We just don't understand it – you have seen the fences and gates. Not even a fit and strong man could get through those unaided."

Annie looked hopefully at Dr Cavendish.

"Do you think she might come here?"

The doctor shook his head dismissively.

"No, that seems most unlikely, Annie. How on earth would she get to Fenton? There's the Wentham to cross and, besides, it has been seventeen years or more since we took her in. No, I would say that was definitely not a possibility that I would want you ever to consider. However, is there anywhere you think that Mary might have gone to? Is there any place near Canford that was special to her while she was growing up and which might still hold memories for her, despite her mental state?"

"No – as far as I remember, we never went across the river when she was with us. Only Gabriel and his father ever used to go there on fishing trips."

"Well," said Dr Cavendish with a sigh. "It's a real mystery to all of us at the asylum, but I think you should be aware of what most people are saying."

"What?" asked Annie, even though she knew what the doctor's answer would be.

"That she has fallen in the Wentham and drowned, Annie."

Annie hung her head and said, quietly,

"No, I don't think that's what has happened. I feel she is still alive."

"Well, we will keep looking and the constables will be out all this week, searching the immediate area round Canford. As soon as we know of her whereabouts – and whether the news is good or bad – I will get word to you and Joshua at once."

"Thank you, Dr Cavendish. I'm so sorry that Mary is such a burden to you all."

"She is no burden, Annie; I just hope she is alright and we find her before she does something to herself or others. And now I must go – it is a long drive by way of Hamsden to get back to Canford. I will bid you good morning."

Dr Cavendish made his way quickly out of number 7 South Beach Cottages, leaving Annie with her mind in a whirl. For the next half an hour or more, she paced up and down her kitchen, unable to sit down or concentrate on anything else but her missing daughter. Where had she gone and why? Why, just a month after their visit to the asylum, had Mary taken her leave? Surely, there had to be a connection.

Joshua was home that day just after four – the fishing had been poor – and Annie was on the doorstep to greet him before, as usual, Gabriel left his father to go to his own house. She called to them both from some yards away, unable to control her news any longer. It had been a long day and she had done virtually nothing. Her husband's supper would be late.

"Dr Cavendish has been. Mary's escaped!"

Gabriel trotted forward and held his mother by the arms.

"What did you say about Mary, Ma?"

"She has got out of the asylum and they can't find her."

"What's that?" said Joshua as he reached his wife.

"Mary's escaped," repeated Annie. "You must both go and look for her."

Both men looked at each other with grim and concerned expressions on their faces as they quickly ushered Ma inside the cottage and away from any neighbours that might be listening. It was the kind of information guaranteed to cause, if not mild panic in the area, then, at least, several tongues wagging. Once safely inside, Annie gave an account of Dr Cavendish's news. Gabriel seemed to be more relaxed about the matter than either of his parents, and though Joshua seemed as anxious as his wife, he quickly dismissed the idea of a search that day.

"Well, we can't go today, Ma. It'll be dark by six and, given the wind, it would take over an hour to get to Canford, if that's where we decided to start looking. You said she's been missing for over three days, so God alone knows where she could be by now."

"Father's right, Ma," said Gabriel. "We will start at first light, but, to be honest, I don't know what more we can do if, as you say, the constables are out looking for her."

"You will go, though, won't you?"

"Yes," said Joshua. "We must – for Mary's sake."

Fortunately, Gabriel and Joshua could feel a brisk southerly breeze on their faces as they made their way down to the South Quay just before seven on the Tuesday morning. It was a fine and sunny spring morning; the weather was in complete contrast to the gloominess of their possibly grim mission. After a gentle stroll down to the harbour, they found the South Quay to be largely deserted at such an early hour and they were under way by a quarter to eight. With Gabriel at the tiller and his father tending to the sails, there was little chance to discuss their plan of action. Indeed, they had said little the night before about where they would go, each preferring to keep their own counsel as to the best places to search. Neither of them really held out much hope of finding Mary and their trip said more about satisfying Annie's need for some kind of action than any real belief that they would succeed in their quest. Apart from the normal necessary exchange of instructions to each other while sailing to the mooring at Canford, it was not until they were walking up the jetty that they began to make plans for the exploration, though both of them knew where they would have to start first.

"Well, I suppose we'd better try the woods first," said Joshua. "I would imagine that most of the other obvious and open places have been searched already."

"That'll be a tough job," replies Gabriel. "They stretch a long way north of Canford – virtually all the way to Northwold, and that's at least four miles from the river."

"It's got to be done, though. At least they're only a couple of hundred yards wide for most of the way. We'll try to walk in parallel lines about fifty yards apart and see how far we get in the time, or until we're tired."

This time, they could see that spring had come early to the trees – they were virtually in full leaf. It was going to hinder their visible horizon considerably and staying in sight of each other might also prove difficult. Within ten minutes, they were under the dense canopy; the sun barely peeping through from above. It was uncomfortably warm for the time of year. They ignored the usual well-trodden paths, walking between the trees at some distance apart as Joshua had suggested. The going was relatively easy, as the undergrowth was still recovering from the harsh winter. Calling out every so often kept them in communication with each other when the trees became denser or the ground's undulations obscured their view. Gabriel had chosen to walk with the sea on his right; the boundary of the woods on that side reaching right to the cliff's edge in most places. With his father keeping the left edge of the woods in sight to his left, they made reasonable and organised progress, not stopping to rendezvous, and for a drink of Ma's home-made lemonade, for over an hour. They joined each other in the middle of the wood, as measured roughly in all directions. Both were sweating profusely. Joshua produced the leather flask from his rucksack.

"It's a warm day, son."

"Yes, but I think we must be about half-way," said Gabriel, wiping his brow with his sleeve. "Have you seen anything unusual?"

"No, and you?"

"Nothing – just the sun through the trees to my right."

Joshua glanced to where his son had indicated and he frowned.

"The sun is behind us now and much higher than the trees anyway – it's nearly eleven. It can't be the sun you've seen."

Gabriel looked behind him and into the canopy above. The sun was peeping through roughly as his father had said.

"Then what did I see?"

"Just the sun reflecting off something, I expect – like what you thought you saw when we came before. There's probably something metallic over there," replied Joshua.

"But that was a good mile further back. We'd only just entered the woods then."

"The light can play funny tricks, lad – especially in these woods when it's so difficult to get a clear view of anything. After all, you thought it was the sun."

"I guess you're right," said Gabriel. "Anyway, we'd better start walking again if we're to be back in time for the tide – otherwise we'll be staying this side of the river for the night."

As they moved further northwards, Gabriel kept searching for the mysterious light. He hadn't said anything to his father, but he was convinced that it had not been a reflection. It had been too high up for that – at least at head height. To him, it had looked like the rising sun as it would have appeared early in the morning on a midwinter's day. He had obviously been temporarily disorientated by his surroundings when he'd first given his explanation of the light to his father.

By noon, the woods began to thin and they soon came across a few humble cottages at the northern edge of the wood; they could also see tiny hamlet of Northwold in the distance.

"Time to turn back, Gabriel, lad," said Joshua.

"Aye, right enough – any further and we'll struggle to get back in time," replied his son. "I'm ready for Ma's pie and cheese cob."

They lunched in a small grassy clearing, shaded by the last oak tree on the edge of the woods. Gabriel seemed preoccupied with his own thoughts and little was said between the two men. The morning had proved fruitless and they were not looking forward to their return ramble over the same ground. Gabriel was soon anxious to make a start.

"Well, we may as well get going. This time, I'm going to walk as close to the cliff edge as possible, to keep an eye open for anything below on the beach."

"Just be careful, son," said Joshua. "That cliff path is quite treacherous in places."

"I will."

As they made for their respective routes, Gabriel's mind returned to its preoccupation with the strange light he'd seen earlier. He had deliberately made the suggestion to walk near the edge of the cliffs as his path should take him past where it had seemed to be coming from.

Gabriel became a little nervous as he approached the area concerned, after an hour or more of slow progress along the tricky cliff path where he'd often had to cling onto overhanging branches for support as he stared at the drop to the beach below. Suddenly, the path widened and formed a small clearing, surrounded by tall elders, open only on the seaward side. It seemed impenetrable from any direction other than the cliff path itself. As he stared at the small glade – which was about twenty feet in diameter and almost exactly circular in form – he was immediately reminded of circles in fairy folklore. The ground was bare of any vegetation and looked rock-hard despite the wet and snowy winter. Gabriel's mud-covered boots were testament to the nature of the surrounding woods. It was indeed a strange place. He peered through the trees into the wood – he felt sure that he must have reached the place where he'd seen the light coming from. There was no sign of his father. He walked slowly forward into the centre of the circle. He could hear his heart beating faster as, suddenly, all surrounding noises ceased – not even the waves breaking on the shore could be heard. Gabriel looked down at the rock-like surface. He knelt down on his knees and placed his palms on it gently – the surface was cold to the touch as his hands stroked the dark grey clay-like material. At first sight, it seemed bare of any marks or indentations until Gabriel raised his eyes towards the edges of the circle. There – at either end of a diameter and close to the circle's edge – were two perfectly formed square holes. Measuring about four inches on each side, they were clearly man-made and looked like they had once held large wooden posts of some description. Gabriel put his arm into one and it was swallowed right up to his elbow, without his fingers making contact with the bottom. He stood up and studied the rest of the circle. There were no other signs of man's presence, and as he looked again at the interior edge of the circle, he found it difficult to imagine how anyone could have built any structure on the spot anyway, unless they had climbed the cliffs from the beach – the circle of elders was even more impenetrable than he'd first thought. He returned to the centre of the circle. He found himself shivering with cold – much colder than he'd been all morning, given the humid and claustrophobic atmosphere in the woods. The place was beginning to disturb him and he had an uncomfortable sense that he was being watched – watched by someone he knew, or had known in the past. Though the impression had lasted but a few seconds, he knew who that person had been – his sister, Mary.

When Gabriel eventually caught up with his father, he made no mention of the strange circle and his accompanying thoughts. Just as he hadn't talked about Mary speaking to him at the asylum, Gabriel would keep his own counsel for some time on the two events that seemed to him to be strangely personal. However, he was sure of one thing – he would make it his business to return to the woods and the circle of elders at the earliest opportunity. He would come alone. He just needed to find a reason to cross the Wentham without sparking any unnecessary curiosity in Joshua, and Annie, in particular.

6
Maggie May

1978 had been a year of recovery for Jennifer Compton-Jones and her partner, Gary. It had taken a long time for both of them to come to terms with the tragic loss of their only son, Ed, on his eighth birthday, just before Christmas the previous year. Despite being divorced since Ed had been a baby, their desire to become good parents and to give him the best and most natural upbringing, had brought them back together as a couple just before Ed had reached his seventh birthday. Old arguments, as to whom or what had to been to blame for the break up of their original marriage, had long been put behind them as they sought to comfort each other on the mysterious loss of their son. Though he was still officially recorded as a missing person, it was generally agreed in the small East Anglian seaside town of Fenton-on-Sea that he had probably drowned in the River Wentham and had been washed out to sea while on a birthday treat, fishing with his father.

When Jennifer announced to her husband on Christmas Eve that she was pregnant for a second time, they felt, finally, that they could approach 1979 with some positive hope for the future and put the tragedy of the past behind them. Jenny Compton-Jones had preserved her maiden name after her divorce from Gary Jones, and her parents, Ann and Fred Compton, were ecstatic when Jenny and Gary gave them the news the following day over Christmas dinner at their house, number 38 Fir Tree Close. Jenny's mother was soon in tears – little Ed's disappearance, and presumed death, had not been the only tragedy to befall her family. Her own son, and Jenny's younger brother, Eddie, had disappeared several years before in even stranger circumstances – he had just walked out one Saturday morning from his home in Fir Tree Close never to be seen again.

He had long been officially declared dead, despite no body ever being found. Jenny and Gary's news of a new grandchild brought memories of the 'family curse', as Ann Compton called it, flooding back to her that Christmas Day.

"Oh, how wonderful, Jenny," she sobbed through her tears. "I just hope we can put our tragedies behind us. It will be a new start for you and us all, dear."

"Yes, Mum, and I pray we can be good parents and that she grows up safely. I'm going to do my utmost to make sure that nothing ever happens to her, like …."

"She? Her?" queried Gary. "How do you know we're going to have a girl?"

"I just know, love," replied Jenny and then she paused. "Or maybe it should be, 'I just hope'. Boys have been unlucky for our family, haven't they?"

"I think, like you said, Jenny, love, that we should all pray for the new baby, whatever its sex," said Fred Compton, at last.

"God gives and God takes away, love – no matter how careful we are in protecting them," added Jenny's mum. "We all did everything we could for Ed and Eddie and, like your dad says, we must pray that nothing ever happens to this one."

Margaret Constance Compton-Jones was born on the very last day – and very nearly the last hour – of May, 1979. She was a healthy seven pounds and three ounces and arrived with a few wisps of delicate blond hair. Jenny and Gary had long decided on the first name, should their baby be a girl, but the middle one had been an afterthought by Jenny's mum to highlight her prayers for their granddaughter to live a long and steadfast life. It would not be long until her parents would shorten her name to

Maggie, in memory of their lost son, Ed, whose jet-black hair and pale complexion had earned him, somewhat unkindly, the nickname of the 'little magpie'. Gary sometimes even extended the pet name for their daughter to *Maggie May*, in reference, both to the month of her birth, and the popular song of the early seventies that had been a favourite of Jenny's.

Maggie grew quickly and thrived on the loving attention of both parents as they sought to ensure that no harm would ever befall her. They were, perhaps, a little too over-protective at times, and with no prospect of a second child, she was inevitably spoiled by all those who loved her. By the time of her third birthday, she had started to develop many of her own characteristics, one of which was the ability to chatter almost incessantly; often making little sense as she gabbled away cheerfully. Jenny even became a little worried that her daughter was not going to be able to learn to speak properly without her having some professional advice and training. The birthday celebration, with Jenny's mum and dad in attendance, would also start to highlight, in Jenny's mind, other possible problems that might lie ahead. It started when Gary brought the birthday cake, with two candles alight, through into the lounge from the kitchen at 26 Acacia Avenue.

"Now, Maggie, a big breath," said Jenny. "Daddy – hold the cake close to her."

Jenny held her daughter in her arms as she manoeuvred her into position so that she could perform the traditional act, but Maggie's lips remained firmly closed.

"Come on, Maggie, love," said Jenny's mum. "Be a good girl and blow hard."

But Maggie wasn't going to be a 'good' girl, and with her face clenched in frustration, she threw both arms out and knocked the cake from her father's hands. It fell sideways to the floor and smashed into a gooey mess of icing, jam and sponge; her name split into several unreadable pieces.

"Whoops!" said Gary, with some awkwardness. "That was not supposed to happen. We should have done it at the table."

"Oh, you naughty girl," said Jenny.

Far from dissolving into tears at the embarrassment of her bad behaviour and spitefulness, Maggie said calmly, and rather haughtily,

"Mary doesn't like cake."

It had been about the first real coherent sentence that any of her family had heard her say and they were all taken a little aback, until Jenny's mum broke the silence.

"And who is Mary, Jenny?"

"Oh, that's what she calls her favourite doll. She christened her Mary when she couldn't say her own name properly. Maggie became Mary when she heard the name in the nursery rhyme, '*Mary, Mary, quite contrary …*' I just hope she doesn't call herself Mary instead of Maggie or Margaret."

Maggie had by now buried her head in Jenny's chest, where, with muffled voice, she mumbled, sulkily,

"I wan' dolly. I wan' Mary."

Jenny's patience finally snapped.

"Then you will join her now in your room, where you will stay until you are ready to come down and say sorry, Maggie."

Jenny stood up and, without ceremony, carried her daughter out of the lounge and upstairs to her bedroom. Maggie was silent – still no tears, histrionics or perceived embarrassment at her standard punishment.

"Here, Gary," said Ann Compton. "I'll help you clean up the mess. Fred, fetch me a bowl of warm water."

"Yes, dear," replied her husband. "Better get it up before it stains the carpet. What a naughty girl."

Later that evening, when Maggie had still refused to make some sort of simple apology for her behaviour, Jenny eventually had to put her to bed without even her usual cuddle and bedtime story. Ever since the birthday cake fiasco, she hadn't once cried openly. By the time Jenny went to wake her the following morning, Maggie's smiling face, and three-year-old girlish charm, immediately put the matter to the back of her mother's mind. As she lay in bed, still cuddling her favourite doll, she grinned cheekily and said,

"Mary is happy now, Mummy."

"I'm pleased to hear it, young lady. And how is my little one?"

Mary clutched her doll closer to her face but said nothing.

"We love you, Mummy."

Jenny took her daughter in her arms – the intended reprimand forgotten after her daughter's attempt at an apology. Somewhere in the back of Jenny's mind she knew that Maggie had got away without the matter being reconciled, simply by shifting the emphasis of the issue to her favourite doll.

Later, when Gary returned from work as the manager of his late father's second-hand car dealership in Hamsden, he, too, would fall for his daughter's charms and nothing more would be said about the ruined birthday cake.

Maggie's behaviour improved a little that summer, but she continued to chatter ceaselessly, often quickly blaming any further small misdemeanours on Mary, with remarks like,

'*It was Mary's fault*', or '*Mary says she sorry, Mum*'.

Jenny would just smile, putting it down to Maggie's age and the embarrassment at being corrected. Though placing the blame for being naughty on her favourite doll annoyed Jenny, she had to smile at her daughter's audacity, even partly aiding and abetting her by designing and making a beautiful old-fashioned dress for Mary, with Easter bonnet and mini parasol. Inevitably, Jenny was coerced into repeating her dressmaking skills with a similar outfit for Maggie as well, which she would often wander around the house in, looking exactly like a character out of some Jane Austen novel.

7
Dreams and Schemes

Annie was naturally disappointed when Joshua and Gabriel returned at dusk after their excursion to the woods near Canford. The sail back had been slow with very little breeze to aid them, though, fortunately, the weather had stayed fair and clear with a beautiful sky of all shades of blue through to red. It was definitely a case of: *'Red sky at night, sailor's delight'*. She had clearly been anxious for their safe return as they arrived back, footsore and exhausted, after their eight-mile trek through the woods.

"Oh, thank God," she exclaimed, as her husband entered the small cottage. "Where on earth have you been? It's nearly seven. Did you …?"

"No, Ma," said Gabriel. "We found nothing."

"Nothing, except Gabriel here thought he saw a light in the woods," said Joshua.

"It must have been an illusion," said Gabriel quickly. "Father's right – there was no trace of Mary."

Annie looked sad, but it was clearly the news she had expected to hear and she seemed to quickly recover herself and asked,

"Are you going to stay for your supper, Gabriel?"

"No, Ma. I'd better get back to Naomi and Edward – she'll be as worried as you. I said we'd probably be back by five."

"As you wish, love. She came round here an hour since to see if you'd got back, so I know she was anxious."

With a quick kiss on his mother's cheek, Gabriel bade farewell to his parents. As Annie came back with him to the door, he whispered,

"Don't worry, Ma – I feel sure that Mary is still alive and you will see her again."

Before Ma had a chance to reply or question her son further about his remark, Gabriel had disappeared into the gathering gloom; the sky now a deep fiery red over the calm sea.

Naomi was in tears as her husband returned home ten minutes later, and she had clearly been crying for some time. She rushed into the hall – baby Edward in her arms – as soon as she heard the front door open.

"Oh, Gabriel – I've been so worried. I thought you'd …."

"No, my love," said Gabriel. "The sea was too calm for any tragedies like that. It just took us longer than we thought, with no wind to help us. Besides, Joshua insisted on visiting the constabulary in Canford before we set sail back. He wanted to check to see if they'd found anything."

"And, had they? Did you …?"

"No, to both questions."

"You found nothing?"

"No, my love. It was a difficult day; the woods were thick and it was a long walk and we got almost to Northwold."

As though sensing his parent's disappointment, Edward began to cry and turned his face from Gabriel.

"I'd better put him down," said Naomi. "You look exhausted, love. Go into the parlour and we'll have supper when I come down."

It took Naomi at least ten minutes to settle Edward down and when she returned to her husband, she found him sound asleep in his fireside chair. She didn't wake him and went to prepare her supper alone.

The circle was still there, but it was winter and snow lay thickly on the ground, making it difficult to detect its exact position at first. Gabriel was alone. He had to be careful as the snow had masked the exact edge of the cliff. Within a few seconds, his footprints had almost completely covered the surface and he hardly noticed that the square holes were still visible, despite the several inches of snow that should have filled them in.

"*I told you I'd come back, Ed.*"

"Mary?"

"*Yes, it's me.*"

Gabriel looked all around him – there was no image to the voice and why did it call him by his son's name?

"*Over here, Ed.*"

"Where?"

"*Here.*"

The voice screamed.

"*Here!*"

Still, Gabriel could see nobody.

"*Turn round, Ed!*"

Gabriel turned and looked towards the sea, and there she was. But, like before in a half-remembered dream, it didn't look like his sister. A blond-haired girl of about twenty floated towards him, hovering in the crisp, cold air; her feet just out of his reach.

"Mary?"

"*Yes, of course I'm Mary. Who else could it be, Ed?*"

"But I'm not Ed. Anyway, we call him Edward and he's upstairs, a ...."

It was definitely a case of déjà vu for Gabriel. He said nothing more. This just wasn't right.

"*Please come with me, Edward then, if that's what you call yourself now.*"

"*No,*" mouthed Gabriel, and he shook his head from side to side.

"Please follow me. I can show you things, Edward. Come on, Edward! Come on, Ed!"

The voice was insistent now and Gabriel backed away from the ghostly apparition as he felt his body start to slide towards the cliff edge. He screamed.

"No! You're not Mary! Go away!"

"Come with me, Edward!"

"No! You're not my sister!"

He was sliding over the edge now. He looked down. It was black. There was no sea or beach – just an all-enveloping blackness.

"No!" he screamed. "No! I'm not Edward!"

"Oh, come on, Gabriel – please wake up."

"What? Oh, I …."

"And you're right, Gabriel? I'm not you're sister, love."

"Oh, Naomi, I was dreaming."

"I know, and screaming as well, my love."

"Oh, what did I say?"

"I only heard the last few words – I was in the kitchen. You thought I was Mary, I think, and you said your son's name once or twice."

"Did I?" said Gabriel, now fully awake. He stretched himself in the chair.

"Oh, how my body aches? How long have I been asleep?"

"Only about half an hour. I was just getting my supper. Do you want yours now?"

"Yes, I'm hungry. I haven't eaten since midday."

As Gabriel stood up and continued his stretching exercises, Naomi said,

"What was the dream about?"

Gabriel shook his head. He was thinking quickly.

"I can't remember much. I think I was in some kind of danger and my sister was involved somehow but nothing else comes back to me now," he lied.

"Well, I hope they're not starting again. I suspect it was just today's search for Mary that set you off."

"Yes," replied Gabriel, though he had an awful feeling that his wife's hopes might be dashed in the near future. He could remember virtually every thing he'd seen in his dream, including the worrying fact that the blond-haired 'Mary' had been wearing clothes which were clearly from another age – an age that the currently popular science fiction writer, H G Wells, might have portrayed in his latest novel. In addition, another thing worried that night, and it caused to him to lay awake thinking about it for some time. The blond-haired apparition's opening words had been: '*I told you I'd come back, Ed*', and that was what the real Mary might have said to him after her last remark at the asylum: '*I'll see you again very soon, Gabriel*'. The only difference – and it was a strange and worrying one – was that she had used two different names for him. What did it all mean?

The early part of the summer in Fenton was taken up for most people by the preparations for the up and coming Diamond Jubilee of Mrs Brown, alias Queen Victoria, to be held on June the 22nd. It was going to be a grand affair throughout the country to celebrate the life of a monarch who had reigned longer than anyone else over Britain and the Empire. With the average lifespan of most of her subjects under fifty years at the start of her reign, she had outlived the vast majority of those that had seen her crowned queen in 1837. With Richard Eliott as mayor and Joshua as a senior clerk on the local parish council, both families were to be heavily involved in the town's civic and private celebrations. Indeed, Gabriel's father was always chair of any organising committee for civic affairs – his skills at captaining various fishing and trading vessels during his life had seen him come to the fore in such matters locally.

As a consequence, Gabriel occasionally found himself at a loose end. With his father tied up on council business and Amos disappearing more and more regularly with his cronies to one of the several drinking establishments in the area, the *Richard Goodman* was left moored at the South Quay and no fish were caught. One such day occurred on Tuesday, June the 8th, and, by chance, the opportunity for Gabriel to revisit the woods on the other side of the Wentham presented itself almost naturally. Gabriel had called round to see his father at eight o'clock to see if he was going fishing that day. With Joshua dressed in collar and tie when Gabriel arrived, he knew the answer immediately. But his father had a job for his son. A fellow fisherman and councillor from Canford had some nets he didn't want and had promised them to Joshua at a council meeting the week before. He rarely brought his boat to Fenton, but Joshua, he had said, was quite welcome to come and collect them from his boat moored on the other side of the Wentham. When Joshua asked Gabriel if he would fetch the nets in the *Richard Goodman*, he was surprised at his son's quick and unhesitating agreement to perform the mundane task.

"Are you sure you can manage the boat on your own? Is Amos about today?"

"No – I haven't seen him since we went out last Friday. Anyway, the wind is a nice gentle southerly today and I'll fix the sails for it so I can stay by the tiller."

"Alright, son – we definitely need some new nets. There's more repaired net than original in most of them. The big one always breaks now if there's a large weight of fish, so I bet we're losing a lot through the holes. You've got all day, son, because I'm helping put up the platform and stands for the 22nd outside the town hall."

Gabriel smiled inwardly and asked,

"Are we going to be ready in time?"

"Oh, yes, son – no problem. I suppose you'll be with Naomi and her parents on the day."

"No – I think not, Father. Richard and Mary will be hosting various groups including officiating as the procession goes past the town hall and Edward would only get in the way – not a place for babies, I think. We shall probably come with you and Ma. Will you have to be part of the official celebrations?"

"Oh, no. I'm only a humble councillor who organises and makes things, son. Though I haven't told anyone – I don't want Naomi's father to know just yet – but your mother and I will watch the procession together in the main crowd, even though I'm supposed to be in the civic stand outside the town hall. Then we'll come back to South Beach for the street party – I'm not going to the mayoral lunch afterwards either. It should stretch from the top of the Terrace almost down to South Point. Why don't you, Naomi and Edward join us?"

"I'll mention it to her when I get back later today."

With that, the two men parted and Gabriel made his way down to the South Quay. He was both excited and nervous. He had waited a good few weeks for the opportunity that had suddenly come his way. With no one expecting him back till late afternoon, he had several hours – wind and tide permitting – to explore the mysterious circle near the cliff edge. Naomi would merely assume he was out fishing with his father. As he walked down the cliff path to the harbour, Gabriel planned his day. He could moor the boat, collect the nets, which were apparently just lying on the deck of a boat called the *Canford Spirit*, and then use the rest of the time on his secret expedition. As St Andrew's Church bells sounded the half hour, he estimated he would have at least three hours in the woods, in addition to an hour or so in the Fisherman's Rest for lunch, to give the appearance of normality to the day if anyone should later mention to his father that they had seen him.

When he set sail from the South Quay just after nine o'clock, the wind turned out to be much lighter than Gabriel had anticipated and it took him well over an hour to reach the Wentham. With the tide out too, he found he had to drop anchor for a further hour in order to have enough draught for the *Richard Goodman* to cross the mouth of the river. The mooring at Canford was quite busy and one or two local fishermen passed comment as Gabriel strode up the jetty to the *Canford Spirit*, which lay almost aground at the top end of the jetty.

"What you doing over here, Master Gabriel?"

"A bit out of your way, aren't you, Gabriel Thomas?"

Gabriel did not bother to engage the fishermen in conversation, as it soon became apparent to anyone what his purpose was, and he quickly transferred the nets from the *Spirit* to his own boat. When he had completed the task, he walked back up the jetty and headed inland, trying to ignore several further inquiries.

"Where are you off to now, lad?"

"Got some business in Canford," he eventually replied, somewhat casually.

"What business?" called out one particularly persistent enquirer.

"Still looking for your sister, eh?" said another.

Gabriel said nothing as his stride increased in order to get out of earshot of further queries as to his purpose in Canford. He knew he would have to head directly for the village if he was not to arouse further suspicion, and then enter the woods on a different path than that he had originally intended. Showing his face in Canford would be no bad thing, he thought, given his one reply on the jetty, and he spent half an hour visiting one or two shops, asking some natural questions about their wares. It was noon by the time he managed to make his way to the woods. The day was hot and the flying insects were in abundance when he entered the now dense and leafy forest. It took Gabriel a good while to find the right path that would lead to the strange elder circle, and he was sweating profusely when he finally spied the tall semi-circle near the cliff edge. As he suspected, from memories of his previous visit, it was virtually impossible to approach the circle from the landward side and he had to make a slight detour to enter it via the cliff path.

It was much as he remembered it. The ground was hard and the two indentations were still there, though there was now a fine layer of moss and grass covering the surface of the circle. Given the dryness of the earth, it somehow just didn't seem right to Gabriel. He sat down to wait. He was thirsty but he'd brought nothing with him to drink. The sea was as calm as a millpond and there was not a breath of wind. Everything seemed normal – it was peaceful, and he closed his eyes in anticipation. The ground felt unusually soft, given the hard surface beneath the thin green covering. He lay back and rested his head on his rolled-up shirt, removed earlier in the woods. He was soon fast asleep.

His dream seemed to be a pleasant one. They were playing on the shingle near to South Beach Terrace. Mary was teasing him.

'You can't catch me, Gabriel!'

'Yes, I can, Mary!'

'Oh, no you can't – you're only four and I'm nearly twelve. You're still a baby.'

'No, I'm not. Don't call me a baby!' he shouted.

'Catch me, then!'

Gabriel tried to run after his sister but his little legs wouldn't move. She was running down the beach to the sea.

'Wait for me – I'm coming, Mary!'

Faster and faster she went and still Gabriel was rooted to the spot.

'Come on, Gabriel, the water's warm!' she shouted back.

'Come back, Mary!'

The sea was up to her waist – then her shoulders; her head and then she was gone. Gabriel screamed.

'Mary! Come back!'

Finally, his feet moved and he ran headlong down the shingle, stumbling and falling – falling, falling. Somewhere in the distance he could hear his sister's voice as darkness suddenly descended on his world.

'Come and join me, Gabriel – it's nice here.'

He woke with a start. Bright, warm sunshine hit his face and he was no longer on the beach. Flies were buzzing round his head and ears. He sat up and looked all around him. Mary was not there. She must have ….

The thought came to him after about a minute, as he sat with his knees pulled up to his chin. Surely his dream couldn't mean what he thought it meant? Had Mary drowned after she had escaped? Had it been her ghost he had seen before hovering above the circle? He stood up and walked carefully to the cliff edge. He looked up and out to sea. Would she come again? He waited – minutes passed, but nothing happened. He shaded his eyes from the sun – it had moved to its late afternoon position.

How long had he been asleep? He shook himself. He had to get back to the boat. Mary was not going to come and see him.

"You are not ready yet, Gabriel."

Gabriel turned quickly to look at the trees behind him.

"You can't see me, my dear brother."

"Mary? Where …?"

"Next time, Gabriel. Next time you'll see me and I'll take you with me."

"With you?"

Silence.

"Mary!"

Gabriel rubbed his eyes and peered into the elders. He looked above and around him but Mary was nowhere to be seen that day. The voice had just been inside his head. But what did it all mean? He sat down. What was he not ready for? Where was she going to take him – if he went with her? If, as he suspected, his sister was dead, would that mean he would have to be, too, if he accepted her invitation? It frightened him and he knew immediately that he had to get away from the circle. As he made for the cliff path, he had an awful sensation that he was not going to be allowed to leave it. It seemed difficult to walk. He doubled his efforts and tried to shake his head clear of his thoughts and, to his great relief, it worked and he was soon back on the path, running – running away from the strange and frightening circle. He didn't stop until he was out of the woods and on the track back to the mooring on the Wentham. Once in sight of the jetty, he finally slowed to a nonchalant amble, his relaxed attitude belying the scratches to his upper body; the torn trousers and his leaf-covered hair, as he walked back, bare-chested, to the *Richard Goodman*.

He was quiet that evening when he got back to Fenton. The wind had strengthened and veered into a north-easterly direction, making his return trip both quick and a busy one. He'd had no time to dwell on his dream or the mysterious voice – all his time had been occupied with rearranging the sales as the boat sped across the choppy sea. After stowing the newly acquired nets below, he made his way back home, tired and somewhat confused at the turn of events that afternoon. Though he had clearly been expected earlier when, at seven-fifteen, he opened the front door to be met by his wife holding Edward in her arms, it was not her first concern.

"Goodness, Gabriel – what have you been doing? How did you get your clothes into that state? Have you been fighting?"

"No, lass," replied Gabriel, as he caught a glimpse of himself in the large hall mirror. "The nets were awkward to carry and I fell twice. The seas were quite rough on the way back as well."

"But your face is scratched and your trousers are torn. You didn't do that just carrying the nets, my love."

Gabriel tried to persist with his explanation but soon realised that it sounded inadequate even to him and he would have to tell the truth – Naomi knew him too well. He stood in front of her and held her arms firmly. Edward started to cry.

"No, I didn't, Naomi."

"Well? What have you been doing?"

"First, you make me a promise."

"What?"

"Promise me you won't tell my mother or father what I've been doing today."

"I can't if you don't tell me first."

"Promise me, Naomi."

"Why?"

"Because it concerns Mary."

Naomi shifted Edward in her arms and gasped,

"Have you found her?"

"No."

"Then what?"

And then Gabriel told his wife as much as he felt able to or, indeed, wanted to. Yes, he had gone over the Wentham to look for Mary but, no, he hadn't found her. He had laid down to rest and must have fallen to sleep. He must have dreamed or heard voices in his head, he thought. Then he had got scared and had fled back through the overgrown woods, ignoring the brambles and branches that were in his way. He didn't mention the strange elder circle or the indentations in its mossy surface. Naomi smiled – she seemed to understand. Her husband had tried to find his sister on his own and had been frightened in the woods. His emotional state had let his mind run away with him. Edward stopped his crying and allowed his father to hold him his arms.

"You must have a hot tub, Gabriel. You look exhausted."

"I am, my love – it has been a trying day."

"Now you make me a promise, Gabriel."

"Anything, my beloved."

"Promise you will never go and try to find Mary on your own ever again."

Gabriel hesitated.

"Promise me, Gabriel."

His sister's words echoed in his head.

'*Next time, Gabriel. Next time you'll see me ....*'

There was going to be a next time, of that Gabriel was certain, and it sounded like Mary was going to make the next contact, too. Little did he know that it would only be a matter of a few days until she put in another appearance, and it would be in unusual circumstances as well. He quickly made his promise.

"I promise you, Naomi that I won't go and look for Mary."

Naomi reached up and kissed her husband. Edward made a gurgling sound and placed his face against his father's. Gabriel smiled and felt warm inside. Naomi said,

"He loves you, Gabriel."

"I do believe he does," said her husband. "At long last, I do believe he does."

8
A Stranger in the Crowd

Despite his promise to Naomi, Gabriel felt that he might still be able to visit the woods near Canford again, as long as he did not attempt the exploration alone. Finding the opportunity and someone to accompany him might prove difficult to arrange, and it would also depend on how long he was prepared to wait for his sister's promised visit to him. But, in his heart of hearts, he was determined to discover, one way or the other, what mystery lay behind his sister's apparition and strange words.

After his abortive visit to the elder circle, the days following were spent both by Naomi's and his family on the last minute preparations for the Diamond Jubilee celebrations on the 22nd of the month. Gabriel, Joshua and, occasionally, Amos went out fishing on the *Richard Goodman* only about every other day. The remainder of Joshua's time was involved with his role in organising the seating arrangements and the like for the main stands outside the town hall, whilst Gabriel spent much of his time helping fit out the display representing the local fishing community, which would be transported on a horse-drawn carriage in the main procession through the town. The crowds were expected to be large, given it was high summer and people would be flocking into Fenton from the villages for miles around. While Joshua was supposed to have a reasonably senior position in the stand outside the town hall, his wife, Annie, had not be accorded a similar privilege and it was still a matter of some debate where she and, indeed, Gabriel, Naomi and Edward would be on the day itself. Mayor Richard Eliott and his wife would, of course, be the chief dignitaries, with their seats – or thrones as Naomi was prone to call them – in the very centre of the wooden stand. Two days before the day, Gabriel, Naomi and Edward had joined Naomi's parents for Sunday lunch at *Fair View* and the conversation over their roast beef meal soon centred on the controversial seating arrangements. Naomi was first to broach the awkward subject.

"Father, I just don't think it's right that Annie doesn't have a seat next to Joshua."

"I'm afraid it's tradition, Naomi, that councillors do not have their wives with them on civic occasions. Only the mayor is allowed that privilege."

"Well, it's about time it was changed, that's all I can say. After all, if it wasn't for Edward, even I and Gabriel would be allowed seats."

"You're my daughter – that's why," said Richard Eliott with some pride.

"Anyway," interjected Naomi's mother, "you and Gabriel will enjoy it more by being in the crowd to watch the procession. It's so formal in the main stand."

"Yes, Mother, and we intend joining Gabriel's mother and father for the street party down at South Beach Terrace afterwards, too."

"Oh?" said Richard Eliott, with some surprise. "You know you're invited to the dinner in the town hall after the procession."

"And what am I suppose to do with Edward, Father?"

"I can make arrangements for someone to look after him, my dear."

"No," said Naomi, firmly. "He stays with Gabriel and me."

"Just as you wish, my dear, but I think you'll find that Joshua is invited to the civic dinner."

Gabriel had remained silent up to this point – not even his wife was aware of Joshua's intentions for the day – and he said quietly,

"My father has decided not to go to the dinner or take his place in the stand – since Annie is not invited, Richard."

There was an awkward silence for a few seconds until Naomi said,

"Well, I think the whole occasion is a bit of a shambles. I mean, tradition is one thing, but when it splits up families for the day, it really is intolerable."

"That may be, Naomi, but you will find that it is done like that up and down the country and these traditions are important to small towns like ours. We feel part of the bigger whole."

"We're hardly a town, Father – more of a village I'd say. How you can call that building a town hall, I'll never know? It's no more that a village hall."

"The parish council decided on that to attract more business to the *town*."

"Well, I think it's a lie, Father," said Naomi, crossly.

Richard Eliott looked sternly at his daughter and said,

"You had better be careful what you say, my daughter – you have an important and privileged position in local society and don't you forget it."

"So?" said Naomi, sulkily.

"That's enough, Naomi," said Mary Eliott. "Your father is right. We have to uphold traditions and back decisions taken by the council. You should know your position."

Naomi was about to retort but Gabriel reached across the table and held her wrist firmly. She tried to remove her hand but Gabriel's grip was firm. The tension was suddenly relieved by Edward crying from his crib in the corner of the Eliott's dining room and Gabriel released his grip to allow his wife to attend to their son. Picking Edward up, Naomi quickly made her way out of the dining room while Gabriel stayed with her parents to finish his meal. Hardly a word was spoken until Naomi returned with Edward asleep in her arms. Placing back in his crib, she returned to her seat at the table and said, quietly,

"I'm sorry, Father, for what I said. I do know how privileged I am."

Richard Eliott smiled his acknowledgement at his daughter's contrition, even though he was unaware that it was not entirely sincere. She was learning that acquiescence in such matters was sometimes a better ploy than arguing pointlessly against her father and his outmoded ways, as she regarded them.

The big day arrived with weather to fit the occasion – not too hot and a gentle breeze to keep the dignitaries in their finery cool and relaxed, given the inevitable tension caused by everyone's concern that the procession and other civic events should proceed smoothly. Gabriel and Naomi, together with Edward in his pram, made the short walk to call for Annie and Joshua at ten-thirty. By ten to eleven, they had taken up a position opposite the 'town' hall from where they would all watch the procession which was due to start at eleven. Naomi waved to her mother in the stands opposite, but could not make out her father until the main civic party took their places just as St Andrew's clock struck the hour. Somewhere in the distance a band could be heard striking up a well known marching tune – the procession was on the move from the station forecourt at the top of the High Street, where it had been assembling since before nine o'clock. An almost audible sigh of relief emanated from the small crowd of civic dignitaries and guests opposite – the celebrations had begun. The main crowd murmured, too, but less from an easing of tension and more out of natural excitement – nothing had been seen like the day's procession in years in Fenton, or for miles around. There was an expectant hush when, five minutes later, the sound of hooves could be heard rattling against the road surface. The crowd around Gabriel pushed forward, rocking the pram. Naomi had to hold its handles tight to avoid it being overturned.

"Steady, lass," said Gabriel to one young lady as she brushed past to get a better view at the front. She turned back and said,

"Sorry, Ed."

Gabriel watched, open-mouthed, as the blond-haired girl forced her way onto the front row. He glanced nervously out of the corner of his eye at Naomi to see if she had heard what the girl had said, but it was clear from her expression and those from his parents that he had been the only one to have heard the girl speak. His mind was in a whirl, and with Naomi trying to say something to him, he was at a loss as what to do. The girl in front of him now – not ten feet away – had sounded like his sister, but the face and hair had been someone else's. They belonged to the girl he had seen in his dream once before on the *Richard Goodman* – the girl that his father had called Mary, even though Gabriel had known then that she wasn't – indeed couldn't be, his sister. He studied her long blond hair. He had to go and talk to her, but how? Finally, he heard what his wife was saying to him.

"I said – do you want to go to the front, Gabriel?"

"Maybe in a minute, when the procession comes past."

"Well, it looked like you were trying to get there, love. Do you know that girl, then?"

Gabriel's swarthy cheeks reddened. Had it been that obvious that he had been staring at the girl?

"No – of course not, Naomi. I just thought she was a bit rude pushing past like that."

"Yes, she was," said Annie. "She stood on my toes."

"She looks a strange one, that girl," added Joshua. "Never seen clothes like hers before."

"Maybe a gypsy from the country, dear," replied Ma. "I thought she seemed to know you, though, Gabriel. Didn't she say something to you?"

"She just said, excuse me, I think, Ma," said Gabriel nervously. "I wasn't really listening."

Suddenly, the leader of the band came into view and Gabriel breathed a sigh of relief as the girl was no longer the focus of their conversation. He looked towards the front row, but the girl had gone, and no matter in which direction he turned, there was no sign of her blond head. She had vanished into thin air.

9
Through the Portal

Though the rest of the celebrations that day passed off without further alarm for Gabriel, his subsequent quietness did not go unnoticed by his wife. With the street party in full swing by three o'clock, and Edward asleep in his crib at Joshua and Annie's cottage, Naomi had time to talk to Gabriel about his apparent lack of interest since the parade. The afternoon was warm as she sat down beside her husband outside number 7 South Beach Terrace.

"Now, Gabriel, what is the matter with you?"

Gabriel's eyes were focused on the distant horizon out to sea and he seemed not to hear his wife's question.

"I said, what's been the matter, Gabriel?"

"Oh, what?"

"Really, Gabriel! You *are* in another world. What have you been thinking about?"

"Oh, nothing. I guess I'm just tired, my love."

"Tired? You've had nothing to do all day, Gabriel. How can you be tired? And you haven't had a drink either."

Gabriel was about to reply when Joshua joined them carrying two large jugs of ale.

"Here you are son, a celebratory drink to her majesty."

"Yes, Father-in-law," said Naomi curtly, "I think Gabriel could do with some refreshment. He seems listless and ill at ease for one reason or another. See if you can find out what's wrong with him while I go and chat to Annie and her friends."

Naomi stood up and moved away leaving the two men to drink their beers in the sunshine. Neither said anything for a few minutes as their thirsts dominated their immediate thoughts. Joshua had also sensed that his son had been preoccupied since before lunch and, consequently, he was hesitant when he broached the subject of his son's vagueness.

"Now, Gabriel, have you enjoyed the day so far?"

"Yes – the parade was a fine affair. Our float was magnificent," replied his son, unemotionally. Joshua probed deeper.

"Did you not sleep well last night, then?"

Gabriel knew what his father was hinting at and he tried to divert the conversation.

"I may have dreamed a little, but my demeanour is probably due to my lack of food. I had little breakfast this morning. We had so much to do to get ready for the procession and Edward was crying a lot, both last night and first thing today."

Gabriel's father looked at his son with a curious grin.

"Well there is plenty of food in front of you on the tables, son. You've had ample opportunity to eat."

"I know but I'm just not hungry. Maybe I'm coming down with something."

Joshua smiled at his son's apparent contradiction and said,

"Well, whatever it is, it has not affected your ability to imbibe your ale, son – your tankard is already empty. Shall I fetch you another? Looks like you need it."

"Yes, it may help me feel better."

Gabriel's father rose and disappeared into the cottage to refill their tankards with his home-made special brew. His son lay back in his chair and closed his eyes against the sun's glare. His mind was still in turmoil after the encounter with the strange girl in the crowd. Mary had said she would appear for real again: *'Next time you'll see me and I'll take you with me'*. Those had been her words, hadn't they? However, Gabriel was not altogether certain that he had actually seen her this time. If it had been Mary, why hadn't she taken him with her, as she had said she would? What did it all mean? How was she going to take him, and when? Above all, Gabriel's mind was troubled by one question: Why had Mary looked like a complete stranger, not only physically but of a different age, too? Why had she been wearing clothes the like of which he had never seen before? As he opened his eyes at his father's return, he suddenly realised that, apart from her hair and her age, it had been the clothes that had bothered him most. They had been from another age, appearing ultramodern and unseemly for a young girl living in the last few years of the nineteenth century. Just as his father was about to say something, a final thought came to him. If the girl wasn't his sister, who was she?

"Here we are son – these will quench your thirst and lighten your mood."

Gabriel's eyes opened wider as he saw his tankard of foaming ale accompanied by a small tumbler of an amber liquid that could only be his favourite *usquebaugh*. He noticed that his father's tankard had a similar addition and for the first time since the procession Gabriel began to relax, putting his earlier thoughts well to the back of his mind.

"Your very good health, Father. You deserve to celebrate after all your efforts to make today a success for Fenton."

"Thank you, Gabriel, I'm glad it's over and I can return to being a humble fisherman tomorrow."

"You'll never just be a humble fisherman, Father. Too many people in the town rely on you."

With his father absorbing his son's compliments to the full, it soon became apparent that both men had every intention of enjoying their ales and whiskies for some time that afternoon – one out of pride and relief at a successful day, and one out of the need to blank his mind of strange and worrying thoughts.

Father and son continued to drink until the sun had almost set, despite several attempts by Naomi and, to a lesser extent, Annie, to curtail their bacchanalian excesses. The warm sunshine had given them excuse enough, if one had ever been needed, to continue imbibing and it was only when the last of the neighbours had left the street party that the two men ceased their drinking, not least because the whisky bottle was empty and their stomachs had no more capacity for Joshua's foaming ale. Their condition was such that neither man was any use in tidying up the tables, chairs or all the remaining food and plates, causing Annie to remark with some anger,

"You two had better make yourselves scarce and make for your beds – you're good for nothing in this state. And, Gabriel, Naomi has taken Edward and gone home an hour since. She was tired of trying to stop you and your father drinking. I suspect you will not be in your own bed tonight, young man."

Joshua was much better able to stand than his son who tried the manoeuvre once, only to fall back into his chair with a clatter. Annie then tried to help her husband get Gabriel vertical but after the third attempt, she said,

"You had better stay here for the night, son. You can't even stand, let alone walk."

"Ah, lea' him be, Ma," said Joshua, slurring his words. "Let 'im sleep there."

And so it was that Gabriel was left where he was, in his chair, the final rays of the setting sun gleaming off his ruddy face, now bathed in alcoholic perspiration. Within five minutes, he was in a seemingly impossible deep sleep, given the uncomfortable nature of the wooden hard-backed chair he sat in.

It was unbearably hot in the woods; yet it didn't seem to be high summer. The leaves were a withered brown and the undergrowth crackled underfoot, indicating it was late autumn. The warmth of the day seemed to be at odds with his surroundings but Gabriel knew what he had to do – what he was supposed to do. Mary was calling for him in his head – silent but insistent.

'*Come and join me, brother. It's fun here.*'

Gabriel stumbled blindly forward, not knowing in which direction to go but it didn't seem to matter. He wasn't in control of his legs and he was being guided by an unknown power.

'*Come, on, Gabriel. Be quick now – it's time to join us.*'

Still Gabriel lurched onwards, ignoring the possibility that Mary seemed not to be alone. He felt warm inside at the prospect at seeing his sister again, made all the more exciting by the fact that she sounded quite sane; just like she had been when he had been a boy and they had played on the beach near South Beach terrace.

'*Not much further now.*'

And suddenly, there it was in front of him – the glade of elders. Gabriel tried to increase his pace but without success as the unseen power was in complete control and led him smoothly and steadily forward. As he joined the cliff path, he hardly noticed that the elders were in full leaf – lush and green in their late spring cloaks.

'*Come into the circle, dear brother.*'

Suddenly, almost as if the invisible power knew that it had finished its task in getting him to the ring of elders, Gabriel felt in control of his movement again and he walked boldly into the fairy circle. However, he quickly stopped before he reached the centre, as his path was now blocked by a most unusual structure – a structure that went some way to explaining the square holes in the ground he'd seen before. He looked upwards at what appeared to be an archway built on two enormous square pillars fixed into the ground about eight feet apart and standing about the same distance tall. The arch was semi-circular and towered a good twelve feet above the ground at its highest point. It was aligned parallel to the line of the cliffs and appeared to be constructed of pure white stone. This strange edifice seemed to have no purpose, being unattached to any building that might have needed it. It was also devoid of any markings to indicate its origin. Incredibly, given the engineering needed to build it, it was made of one piece of the marble-like stone with no visible signs of any joins. It was one continuous piece of architecture. Gabriel stood in awe at its splendour.

'Now you have to pass through the portal if you want to join us, Gabriel.'

Gabriel looked behind him, and there she was – the Mary he had known when he had been six, her long black hair billowing in the breeze as she floated above the edge of the cliff just above head height. She looked fourteen again and Gabriel felt happy. They were going to play their favourite games on the beach, weren't they?

'Go round the side of the portal and enter from the other side, brother.'

Mary's voice was more insistent now and there was an edge to it he'd never heard before. It wasn't just an invite any longer – it was a command and Gabriel found himself obeying it without question as he walked round the left-hand pillar. As he passed, he put out his hand for support and touched the white stone column. It was cold – icy cold and felt more like wood than the solid stone it had looked like at first sight.

The pillar was rougher than he had thought it to be with a grain-like quality to surface. His gentle touch even seemed to set the strange portal swaying, causing Mary to call out,

'*Be quick now, the portal will soon disappear. You should not have touched it, Gabriel.*'

Gabriel had reached the inward entrance to the gateway where he then hesitated briefly.

"*Quickly, Gabriel! Oh please be quick*!'

Mary's voice screamed above the noise of the waves below, simultaneously drowning out any last minute fears that might have still been lingering inside his head. He stepped forward and walked through the portal where the unseen force once more took over as he stepped, without further hesitation, over the edge of the cliff.

'*Hurrah! Gabriel's here at last.*'

Mary's voice was the last thing he heard as blackness descended on his world. Apart from her words, the only other thing to impinge on Gabriel's mind was sheer terror at the imminent certainty of serious injury or even death as he braced himself for the inevitable encounter with the hard shingle fifty feet below. That impact never came.

When light returned to Gabriel's world, and he realised he could feel no pain or discomfort, his ears were the first of his sensory organs to take in his new surroundings. At first, with the light so bright, visual interpretation of those sounds proved difficult. The ground felt soft to his feet and it was clear to him his was close to the sea but above the noise of the waves he could also hear the sound of children's voices.

"*Come on, Ed, let Maggie have a kick!*"

"*Yeah, I wanna' go.*"

Finally, Gabriel looked around himself and he realised at once that the voices had been directed at him. But why had they called him Ed, after his son. Mary was nowhere to be seen; just two children – a boy of about eleven and a girl aged about three or four. She was unsteady on her feet, and on the sandy beach – for that's where Gabriel decided he must have landed – she was continually falling over. Both children had beautiful blond hair. He looked down at his own feet, and the first thing he noticed was that his corduroy trousers had been cut short above his knees and were of a lighter cotton material. His heavy brogue shoes had been replaced by white sandshoes of a canvas-type material. A brightly coloured ball lay beside his feet. He had never seen any such a thing before in his life. It seemed to have small union jacks painted onto its surface at regular intervals. The blond haired boy spoke again.

"Come on, Ed, old son, give us the ball."

Gabriel lifted his eyes to study the boy more carefully. He was tall and quite sturdily built bordering on being obese and had a ruddy complexion and unkempt hair. Gabriel said nothing and turned to look at the little girl. Though she had only said a few words up till then, her voice had sounded like a younger version of his sister's. He tried to mouth her name but no words came out. He moved his foot and the ball shot across the sand even though he felt no sensation. The two children seemed satisfied and the little girl scampered after it while the boy approached Gabriel with a quizzical look on his face.

"Where have you been, Ed? Everyone's missed you. Do you fancy coming up to the farm later."

The boy was in front of him now but still Gabriel found himself unable to speak. The boy continued.

"Don't you remember me, Ed? It's your old friend Minor and that's your sister, Maggie, over there, mate, but you won't have seen her before, will you? We're all happy now. We have fun all day long and we never have to go home."

'Minor' paused.

"Unless we want to that is, of course."

Still Gabriel's mouth remained firmly shut. He wanted to ask this boy questions and to tell him that his sister was called Mary, not Maggie, and that she had black hair like his. He felt the frustration welling up inside him. The boy came closer so that his face was barely inches from his own. And then Gabriel realised what was really wrong about his new situation. With Minor's eyes looking *down* into his own, he knew it could only mean one thing – he must be smaller than this unknown boy. He must look like a child again. The girl called Maggie returned with the ball in her arms and joined the two 'boys'.

"Ed, kick it again," she said, coyly.

Maggie passed the ball to Gabriel and that single motion told him that he wanted no further part in the nightmare. Instead of lifting her arms up to his, as if he were the roughly the same age and height as the boy, she merely moved them forward on the same level as her own. In that instant, Gabriel felt his body regain its own power to obey his brain's instructions and he turned and fled away across the sand.

'*Come back, Ed*! *Come and play with us!*'

He ignored the children's cries and headed up the beach, all at once realising that he was back in Fenton and not below Canford woods. He could see St Andrew's Church above him, but something was wrong. Where was the cliff path? He stopped and took in more of his surroundings. Directly in front of him was a stone-looking promenade which stretched both north and south below the cliffs. The cliffs had been turned into gardens with paths and shelters. Then, for almost the first time since his nightmare began, he remembered how he'd got there. Where was Mary?

Suddenly, the power of speech returned and Gabriel cried out,

"*Where am I? What has happened to Fenton?*"

He felt cold and his body was aching.

"*Help me – where am I? Where is Mary? Oh, God, where am I?*"

"*Now stop shouting, son. You'll scare the neighbours. You're where we left you and Mary is gone.*"

The familiar voice rang in his ears. He tried to move but stiffness had taken over his body. He opened his eyes. It had all been another dream. Ma was standing in front of him, gently rubbing his hands.

"Come on, son, wake up. You had too much to drink and you're cold enough for the grave. Your father is sound asleep and I can't lift you by myself. You'll have to try to stand on your own. Naomi will be worried sick – it's gone eleven."

"What? Oh – I'm so cold, Ma. Just give me a moment and I'll be alright."

Ma stood back and watched as Gabriel lifted himself out of the chair and stood in front of her. She held out her arms expecting him to fall over but instead, Gabriel held out his own arms and smiled.

"I'm fine now, Ma – jut a bit of a headache."

Ma then watched in amazement as her son walked unaided for a few yards, thus demonstrating that his body was clear of its alcoholic stupor.

"Well, you've no right to be, Gabriel. You deserve to be punished for the amount you have drunk today."

"Honestly, I'm fine, Ma, and if you don't mind, I'll be on my way back home now."

With that, and with Ma's wide open in astonishment, Gabriel walked off into the darkness, lit only by the full moon overhead. Though he could not remember his entire dream as he walked home alone, the experience had been sufficient to cure any hangover that the drink should have otherwise have given him. Above all, his mind was in turmoil over his sister's appearance in his dream. Why had she led him through the portal with such excitement in her voice only for her not to be on the 'other side'? Unless, of course, she had taken on the appearance of the little blond haired girl who, along with her unknown friend, appeared to be living in another time – a time that was probably many years in the future. Was the little blond girl the same person as the young woman he'd seen both at the procession and previously in another dream? And who was the boy who had called himself Minor? The name seemed to be familiar to Gabriel from some long forgotten dream from his past when he'd had his 'illness'.

He slept that night on the sofa in the parlour, having not dared to wake Naomi who had already retired when he eventually got home just before midnight. Arguments and recriminations would have to wait till the morning. Other thoughts would dominate Gabriel's mind during the early hours of the following day and a dreamless sleep would only return just before dawn when his mind finally succumbed to his body's need for rest from its dark wanderings which were full of contradictions and impossibilities. Of those impossibilities, the one that plagued his mind the most and caused him the most worry was his own apparent physical appearance in the dream. He had been a child, of that there was no doubt, but he must have been very small for his age and why had they called him Ed? It just didn't make any kind of sense, especially as he recalled the boy's words about his supposed sister: '... *that's your sister, Maggie ... but you won't have seen her before ....*' That was nonsense, surely? He *had* seen his sister before or, at least, he had seen *Mary* before, and so who was the girl called Maggie? It was an impossible jumble of apparently unconnected facts and events and the only thing that provided any semblance of comfort for Gabriel that night was the knowledge that dreams often provided visions of impossible connections about people, places and times. That's what dreams were all about, after all. The worrying aspect from Gabriel's point of view was that his dreams seemed to have some kind of consistency running through them where the same unknown people and places kept recurring with strange regularity.

10
Tantrums

By the time the Christmas shopping season arrived in 1983, little Maggie Compton-Jones' behaviour, especially in public, seemed to have improved somewhat – so much so that Jenny felt able to take her to Hamsden on her own to see Father Christmas in his grotto at Osborne's department store. The four-year-old was really excited by the prospect and on the last Friday before Christmas, she seemed barely able to control her emotions at the breakfast table with her mum and dad. It had only just turned eight o'clock.

"I don't want any breakfast, Mum. I want to go and see Santa now."

"We're going at half past nine, love," replied Jenny, suspecting from her daughter's tone that she was about to have one of her old tantrums. She was pleasantly surprised when Maggie said,

"Yes, Mum. I'm a good girl, aren't I?"

"Of course you are, Maggie."

"Right, I'm off to work," said Gary, clearly relieved that he felt he could leave his daughter in Jenny's capable hands. "I'll see you both at lunchtime. Come to the showroom at one, Jen, O.K?"

"O.K.," said Jenny. "Lunch at the Old Market Restaurant if this young lady is good."

Maggie smiled and returned to eating her cornflakes while Jenny kissed her husband goodbye.

Exactly an hour later, and several minutes earlier than planned, Jenny put her daughter into her car seat in the back of her new red Ford Escort and headed for the shops in the neighbouring town of Hamsden, twelve miles away.

The town was busy – busier than Jenny had expected and she ditched the idea of taking Maggie in her old, and now rarely used pushchair. She just couldn't face negotiating the crowds with it and, as they left the car, she made Maggie promise to keep hold of her hand all the time. She would only be carried, she said, if it proved absolutely necessary. Maggie made the appropriate promise.

"I'll be good, Mummy."

Jenny knew that if she took her daughter to Osborne's at the start of the morning she would quickly become bored for the rest of the morning – delaying the visit to Father Christmas would hopefully preserve Maggie's excitement.

"Right, I want to go to Taylor's first for one of Daddy's presents, Maggie."

"Yes, Mum," replied her daughter, politely.

Jenny looked down at her daughter with a curious smile.

"Are you alright, love?"

"Yes, Mum."

This was too good to be true, thought Jenny. Was this the lull before the storm? She hoped not as she took her daughter's hand to make the walk through the gathering crowds. It was still not ten o'clock. It could be a long morning until reinforcements, in the shape of Gary, arrived. Jenny's 'battle' had commenced.

The first skirmish didn't take place until Jenny had selected a rather nice silk tie for Gary on the top floor of the upmarket tailors with the appropriate name. The shop assistant was just about to wrap it when Maggie bawled,

"I don't like red. Daddy doesn't like red. Mary doesn't like red."

Jenny gripped her daughter's hand more tightly and said,

"Shh, Maggie – of course he does. Why do you think he bought my red car? Besides, you left Mary in the car."

That seemed to be the trigger for the first onslaught as Maggie then screamed at the top of her voice,

"I want Mary! Go and get Mary!"

The young male assistant, sensing Jenny was about to have her hands full, tried to distract Maggie.

"Would you like a sweetie, young lady?"

"No!" came the shouted rely. "I want my dolly!"

The assistant hastily completed the gift wrap and Jenny handed over a five-pond note. She didn't wait for the fifty pence change as she grabbed the present and pulled her daughter away from the counter.

"Right, no Father Christmas for you, my girl. You've been very naughty."

They had reached the down elevator by now and Maggie suddenly stopped walking and said,

"Sorry, Mum. I *am* a good girl."

Jenny could hardly believe her hears. How could her daughter change her emotions so quickly? Her face had gone from frustrated anger to calm humility in a couple of short minutes. It was almost like she was using a tap that she could turn on and off at will. Jenny was caught totally off guard and she stammered,

"Tha-at's alright, love. We'll go somewhere nice now. Shall we have a drink and a doughnut in Pritchard's Coffee House?"

"Ooh, yes please, Mum."

As they took their places on the elevator, Jenny failed to notice the sly grin that appeared on her daughter's face – a grin that said: '*I know how to get my own way. Mummy knows that doughnuts are my favourite.*'

The initial skirmish became a full-blown attack after Jenny had escorted Maggie to Hamsden's premier coffee house and cafeteria opposite Taylor's. Some thing or someone had turned the tap full on again and this time the screams would be accompanied by a battalion of tears. Jenny had hardly finished the purchase of two large jam doughnuts, a cappuccino and a fizzy orange when, for no apparent reason, Maggie burst into another caterwaul.

"I want a coke!" she screamed.

Jenny was taken aback by the suddenness and ferocity of the verbal assault. She tried to stay calm.

"Now, Maggie, I've told you before – Coca-Cola is not good for you and, anyway, you asked for orange."

"Mary doesn't like orange!"

Jenny's patience was beginning to wear thin.

"I've told you already that you left Mary in the car – and stop using her as an excuse for everything you say. I'm really getting fed up with it, Maggie."

The drums started up.

"I wan' Mary! I wan' Mary! I wan' Mary!"

A few people from neighbouring tables were now taking notice of Maggie's histrionics and Jenny could not fail to overhear one or two comments being made in the background.

'*She's a spoiled little girl, that one.*'

'*Just because she can't get her own way.*'

Finally, one rather plump middle-aged lady leant over and spoke directly to Maggie herself.

"Now then, dear, Father Christmas won't bring you anything nice if you keep screaming like that."

Maggie said nothing while Jenny watched in horror as a large dark stain suddenly appeared on the front of the lady's white blouse; it had a slight orange tint to it. The middle-aged lady's mouth competed with her eyes to see which could open the widest. Maggie sat back in her chair and scowled. The tap, at least, had been turned off again.

"Oh! What have you done?" spluttered the lady, still obviously in shock. "You are a bad girl."

Jenny's embarrassment almost prevented her from responding. She was caught in two minds as what to do for the best – apologise profusely or pick her daughter up and run. She made an attempt at the first.

"Oh, I'm so sorry. I will pay to have that cleaned for you."

"Don't bother," the lady growled. "Just get your daughter out of my sight before I do something I might regret."

Jenny repeated her apology and tried to get her daughter to do the same, but the lady was too busy trying to dry her blouse on a paper napkin to take any notice. With as contrite and humble a smile as she could muster, Jenny lifted her daughter into her arms and walked out of the coffee house as quickly as decorum would allow. Maggie had said nothing since her attack with the fizzy orange missile, merely burying her face in her mother's shoulder. Once outside, Jenny made immediately for the town square where she found an unoccupied bench well away from the main crowds. Despite some mild protestations, she placed her daughter beside her on the wooden seat. It was time for a chat but before Jenny could commence the heart to heart, Maggie said,

"I'm sorry, Mum. Mary says she sorry, too."

Jenny threw eyes heavenward. This was just not happening.

"Oh, Maggie, you just can't keep doing this. Just saying sorry is not enough, child. Whatever were you thinking of in Pritchard's? You can't go round throwing things at people. The policeman will come and lock you up."

"Mary didn't like that lady," said Maggie, quietly.

"Oh, for goodness sake, Maggie. You've got to stop this. I thought you'd got over hiding behind your doll whenever you did anything wrong. I shall have to take you to the doctor – he'll cure you of it, one way or another. And what will Daddy say when I tell him?"

At last Maggie seemed to take notice and she said,

"No, please, Mummy," she sobbed. "I will be good. Please don't take me to the doctor and …."

Now the tears seemed to be real and, for the first time that morning, Jenny thought she could detect genuine penitence in her daughter's face.

"And what?" she asked sternly.

"And don't tell Daddy."

"Then promise me you'll behave for the rest of the morning and I may consider it."

"I promise," she quavered. "Can I still see Santa, Mummy?"

The plea seemed to quell Jenny's anger a little. Minutes earlier, she had made up her mind that Maggie was not going to have that privilege, but something about the tone of her daughter's plea made her say, guardedly,

"We'll see. We'll see."

Battle operations were suspended, but was it going to a permanent armistice or just a temporary lull in proceedings? With a possible visit to Father Christmas in Osborne's still on the agenda, time alone would tell.

Everything went smoothly to begin with at Santa's Grotto in the toy section of Osborne's department store. Maggie sat dutifully and quietly on one knee of a rather fat example of the much beloved Saint Nicholas and neither he nor Jenny was quite prepared for the next assault on their ears. Maggie has just taken possession of the obligatory present from her benefactor when, after tossing the gift aside, she screamed,

"I hate you! Mary hates you!"

Jenny made a grab for her daughter, suspecting matters could get even worse, while a totally bemused Santa bent down to pick up the discarded present. Maggie, however, had no intention of being restrained, either physically or verbally. Quick as a flash, she leapt off Santa's knee and dashed for the exit to the grotto, shouting,

"I want Mary! I want Mary!"

With shock etched all over her face at what she had heard and seen from her daughter, a few vital seconds were to pass before Jenny's brain began to function and she turned to run after her daughter. Santa had to be satisfied with Jenny merely raising her two arms in exasperation for his apology.

Outside the grotto it soon became clear that if Maggie didn't want to be found then Jenny would have little chance of doing just that. The store was packed with Christmas shoppers and spotting, let alone finding, a small four-year-old girl amongst them would be nigh on impossible. Maggie's last screamed words were Jenny's only clue as to where her daughter might have gone and, rather than alerting Osborne's security staff, she headed out of the store to make for the town hall car park.

It took her less than five minutes, despite the thronging crowds in the High Street. Several bewildered shoppers shouted after her to mind what she was doing but Jenny didn't hear their calls. She was in a blind panic, not knowing whether she had made the right decision to head straight for her car. Shouldn't she have stayed in the store and told someone? What if someone had snatched her? Suddenly, she was in the wide open space of the municipal car park. She hesitated. Where had she left the Escort? Then she saw it, its red bodywork glinting in the low December sun. Narrowly missing a car leaving its parking space, she dodged the other parked cars until a few seconds later she reached her target. Twice she ran round her car and even knelt down to look underneath its chassis but Mary was not to be found. She tried the doors, but they were still locked as she had left them. Maggie's doll lay next to the child seat. Jenny was just about to run back to Osborne's when she noticed that a young couple had just returned to the car parked right next to hers. The man said,

"Are you alright, love? Have you lost your keys?"

"No," shouted Jenny. "I can't find my daughter."

The young woman came closer and asked,

"What does she look like?"

"Oh," replied Jenny. "She's four and has blond hair. She was wearing a beige coat buttoned to the neck."

"Ah," said the girl. "I think we may have seen her as we came back into the car park."

"Where?" asked Jenny, anxiously.

"Over there near the Market Lane entrance."

The young woman pointed to a spot about fifty yards away at the opposite end on the car park to the one Jenny had returned by. She muttered her thanks and ran, her heart pounding in expectation that her nightmare might be over. And then she saw it – another red Ford Escort, parked in a far corner and beside it, standing almost nonchalantly, her daughter. Jenny shouted,

"Maggie, oh, Maggie!"

Her daughter ran towards her, arms outstretched and shouting,

"Mary's not in the back seat, Mummy! Someone's taken her!"

Maggie dived into her mother's arms, sobbing uncontrollably.

"Mary's gone, Mummy. I wan' my Mary."

Somewhere in the back of her mind Jenny knew she should be remonstrating with her daughter over her antics at the grotto but the sheer relief that flooded her body was too much for her and in a comforting voice, she said,

"Oh, you silly, silly girl. That's not my car, love."

Maggie raised her head and said quietly,

"Please don't tell Daddy. I won't be naughty ever again, Mummy."

The plea, seemingly spoken with genuine contrition, again caught Jenny off guard and without thinking, she said,

"No, I won't tell Daddy."

"Where is our car, Mummy?"

"It's over there, love."

Jenny lifted her daughter into her arms. She tried to strike a balance between the seriousness of the situation and the joy she was feeling inside.

"You were very naughty in Santa's grotto, you know, don't you, Maggie?"

"Yes, Mummy," mumbled Maggie. "I just didn't like Santa and Ma …."

Jenny held her daughter so that she could look directly into her eyes. For the first time since their reunion she spoke in her sternest voice.

"Don't you dare say it, young lady – alright? If you use Mary as an excuse for anything again, I shall take her away from you and give her to a good little girl."

Maggie started to cry again. The town hall clock struck the half hour and Jenny glanced at her watch. It was twelve-thirty. Where had all the time gone? The correct red Escort was suddenly in front of them and a few seconds later Maggie's tears dried up as she held her beloved Mary in one hand while the other was firmly gripped by her mother's. It would stay attached to it until they reached Gary's second-hand car showroom.

The next half hour was to be largely occupied by a penitent little girl revisiting Santa's grotto to apologise to the 'really nice old man', as Jenny called him. Once a grinning Father Christmas had warmly accepted Maggie's mumbled apology, Jenny was finally satisfied that she had fulfilled her parental responsibilities in trying to teach her daughter how to behave in public and the consequences of failing to do so. She felt like she had been through World War 3 and couldn't wait to get to the showroom and the support of Maggie's father.

Though Jenny said very little about Maggie's strange and naughty behaviour when, a few minutes after one, they met up with Gary, she did express her concerns to him later that day after their daughter was safely tucked up in bed. They had spent some time putting the Christmas decorations up in the lounge at 26 Acacia Avenue and by nine they were both ready for a sit-down and a well-earned bottle of wine. It took two large glasses for Jenny to open up about her morning. Her promise to her daughter seemed irrelevant against the worry and anxiety that Maggie had put her through.

"Maggie wasn't very well-behaved this morning, Gary."

"Oh? I thought you said she'd been good when you came to the showroom. She was certainly fine over lunch – a real credit to you, Jen, and a vast improvement from how she used to behave."

"Well, she wasn't when she was with me, Gary – far from it, in fact."

Gary gave his wife a knowing smile.

"Well, I did wonder, love. There was something curiously coy about her face when I asked you how she'd been. She seemed unduly nervous, almost as though you wanted to say something but couldn't for one reason or another."

Jenny got up and sat on the carpet beside her husband. She looked up into his eyes and held his hand as though needing some kind of support or comfort.

"Gary, she was absolutely awful, but you mustn't say anything to her. I promised I wouldn't tell you."

"How, awful?"

And then Jenny told her story, leaving out the details of the purchase of his present from Taylor's. Gary's face winced at each event until finally, he said,

"Oh, you poor thing. You should have brought her straight to me the first time she started screaming in Taylor's, or just taken her back home and rung me. She's very fortunate to have been allowed to have a nice lunch after all that. She's got to learn that she can't behave like that in public."

"I know, but the little madam kept saying she would be good and I thought I could cope."

"What do you think was wrong with her?" asked Gary.

"That's the whole problem – I just don't know. She loves fizzy orange and hates coke, so why she went off about that doesn't make any kind of sense and …."

"And?"

"And red's her favourite colour."

"Red? What's that got to do with anything?"

"Oh, you might as well know. I was buying you a nice red silk tie from Taylor's and she just said she hated red and that Mary did too. She kept doing that all morning – using her doll to support her actions and hiding behind her as an excuse for her bad behaviour."

"She's done that before," said Gary.

"I know but I thought she'd grown out of it. I've a good mind to throw the doll way while she's asleep. Tell her that Mary doesn't like bad girls and has gone to live with someone else."

"Well, why don't you?"

"Because it's her favourite thing and it would probably only make matters worse. No, we'll just have to make her learn the hard way. In the past, we've probably been too lenient with her and spoiled her, or at least, I have. From now on she won't get any treats if she behaves like that again when I'm out with her."

"Shall I talk to her tomorrow?"

"No, Gary. A promise is a promise. Besides, it's Christmas Eve."

Jenny took a sip of her wine and looked down at the carpet. She seemed to be searching for the right words.

"Gary?"

"Yes, love."

"Gary, it was quite frightening, you know, especially in Santa's grotto. It was the one place she'd wanted to go all morning and if you'd seen …."

"Seen what?"

"Her eyes, Gary. They were black with hate for the poor old man and for a few seconds she seemed as though she …."

Jenny didn't finish her sentence and looked nervously up at her husband.

"Why would she do something like that, Gary? It was so irrational. I mean, she'd never seen the man before and he was no different from all the other Santa's she'd ever come across – on television, or in the shops, and yet she seemed to hate him intensely. It was scary, Gary."

Gary said nothing. Jenny looked up into his eyes for confirmation that he'd actually heard what she'd said.

"Gary, at that precise moment, she looked like someone else. Indeed, it felt like she *was* someone else. I just didn't recognise my own daughter. I'd never seen her look like that before. I just hope poor old Santa wasn't looking into her eyes at the time."

Still Gary said nothing. After another gulp of wine, Jenny continued.

"And what makes matters worse is I was scared or just unwilling to do anything about it. I wanted to say something to her when I caught up with her but she seemed to charm me out of telling her off or discussing why she had behaved so badly. It was like she was controlling me – me, Gary, her own mother."

At last Gary responded.

"Jenny, she's only four. How could she control you?"

"I don't know, Gary, but that's exactly how it felt. You should have been there and seen her. I just wish …."

"What, love?"

"I just wish I knew what set her off. It was so illogical, like she was schizophrenic or something, if that's the right term."

"Now you must be exaggerating, Jenny," said Gary, almost laughing out loud.

"It's not funny, Gary," said Jenny, angrily. "Our daughter has two different personalities; one that could charm the hind legs off a donkey, and one that would make your average witch look like Mary Poppins."

Gary tried to take the heat out of the situation. He didn't like the direction his wife's conversation was going.

"Mood swings, Jenny, that's all it was – mood swings."

"Mood swings, my foot! I'm telling you, Gary, your daughter is two different people and the problem is …."

"Yes, Jenny?"

"The problem as I see it, dear husband, is that I don't think either half of her split personality recognises or even remembers what the other half does."

"How do you mean?"

"I mean that when she says she's sorry, she doesn't really know why she's saying sorry."

Jenny paused.

"Because if she did, she would realise how bad she had been and would be shocked by her own behaviour. As I said, it's like she can't recall precisely what she's done."

Gary reached for the wine bottle and said,

"You've gone beyond me now, love. Have some more wine and forget about it. We know what we must do in future. She's just got to learn right from wrong and if we have to punish her then that's what we'll do – alright?"

"Yes," said Jenny, reluctantly. "I suppose you're right, as usual. I'm tired, I guess. Things will seem better in the morning."

"That's my girl," said a somewhat relieved Gary. "Or I'll begin to think that I'm living with two strange women."

Jenny seemed to relax, but the morning's events would continue to haunt her for some time. Despite her husband's calm and measured approach to the issue, she would have a lingering feeling that there could be something radically wrong with her daughter.

11

The Mornings After

Initially, little dialogue took place between Gabriel and Naomi at breakfast on the day following the Diamond Jubilee celebrations. Though she was not openly hostile to her husband, her answers to his questions and remarks were curt to say the least. Being a Wednesday and a weekday, Gabriel was anxious to return to his normal occupation, fishing from the *Richard Goodman*. With her husband about to leave for the South Quay, it suddenly became clear that Naomi had had enough of the stand-off.

"I hope you are absolutely ashamed of yourself, Gabriel."

Gabriel hung his head and tightened his lips.

"What on earth were you thinking about?" continued Naomi. "You promised me you wouldn't drink like that again. When I left with Edward, you were in a dreadful state. I doubt you even knew that I'd gone, so God alone knows what you were like when you eventually got home, which was when precisely?"

Gabriel lifted his head.

"I don't know, Naomi."

"Well, I brought Edward home at nine and he was still awake at eleven; he seemed to want to see you before he went to sleep. He was very upset and he wanted you to say goodnight to him. His routine is all over the place now and he's still sleeping which, frankly, is a good thing, Gabriel, so he doesn't have to hear what I'm saying."

"I'm sorry, love. I ...."

"Sorry, are we? Is that all you can say? Don't you understand the responsibilities of a father? For pity's sake, Gabriel, I had to walk home alone in the dark, carrying your son. Who knows who or what might have been about? Why on earth did you drink so much?"

Before Gabriel could reply Naomi said,

"Your father is as much to blame – encouraging you like he did. The difference is, Gabriel, he doesn't have a baby son to look after."

Naomi paused and then said, sarcastically,

"Or perhaps he does, eh? A twenty-four-year-old son who is still a baby!"

She was shouting now, all her frustrations coming to the fore. Gabriel made to stand up and leave the breakfast table. Naomi pushed him back down into his chair. Gabriel looked shocked at her physical action.

"Steady on, Naomi, love. Just let me try and explain."

"Explain? What's to explain? You got drunk, plain and simple. I don't need explanations."

"But …."

Gabriel knew he had to try to account for his melancholy and vagueness of the day before that had been the major cause of his drinking. Somehow he had to tell Naomi about the blond haired girl in the crowd. How could he make his feelings believable? Despite her apparent disinterest in an explanation for his behaviour, Naomi seemed to sense that Gabriel was about to say something important.

"But what, Gabriel?"

"It was all to do with Mary, love," he said, quietly.

"You're not still worrying about your sister, are you? She's gone, Gabriel, I've told you before – probably drowned, which is for the best and you know it," said Naomi, rather harshly. Her husband looked up into his wife's eyes and replied,

"You remember the girl who stood on Ma's toes when the procession went past?"

"Ye-es" said Naomi. "What about her? As I recall, you said you didn't know her."

Things were getting difficult for Gabriel. Had he said too much? What could he say next? He started cautiously.

"Well, maybe I did know her, love."

"So, who was she, then? I didn't recognise her – I hadn't seen her around Fenton before. I would have noticed that long blond hair."

"You remembered quite a bit about her, then, Naomi?"

"I suppose so – she was quite rude in pushing past us like that. You haven't answered my question. Who was she?"

"Now you promise you won't think I'm stupid or going mad."

"What, again?" laughed Naomi.

"I won't tell you if you're going to rake all that up. I don't like being reminded of that illness."

Realising how serious and nervous her husband looked, Naomi said,

"Alright, tell me and I promise not to poke fun at you."

"She reminded me of Mary."

"But you said Mary had black hair which had gone prematurely grey when you went to visit with your parents. Besides the girl who we saw was much younger."

"I didn't say she *was* Mary, just that she reminded me *of* Mary."

"Are you sure your mind wasn't just playing tricks on you?"

"No."

"So how did a blond haired young girl remind you of your mad sister?"

A tear began to form in Gabriel's eye at his wife's stark description of his sister's condition.

"Don't call her that, love, please."

"I'm sorry, but …."

"It was her voice. It sounded exactly like Mary's did when she was a young girl before they took her. But it wasn't only her voice. She said something to me."

"What – she apologised for pushing past you?"

"No – she called me something."

"What did she call you? Come on, Gabriel, for goodness sake tell me and stop prevaricating."

"I don't want to upset you, Naomi, but she called me Ed. There, that's the whole story."

"Ed?"

"Yes, like our son."

"But we don't call him that. He's Edward to everyone."

"I know, but it was the way she said it – like she knew me and, as I said, she said it in Mary's voice. I'm certain of that."

"And that's why you felt the need to drink to excess?"

"I suppose so."

"Well, I'm not laughing, Gabriel, but I really do think you must have let your mind run away with you. I know you've been thinking about Mary recently. Maybe this girl's voice did sound a bit like your sister's and that sparked an association in your mind that actually just doesn't exist in reality."

"Maybe, but I can't get her out of my mind, Naomi and there is one more thing."

"I thought you said you'd told me everything."

"I had, about the girl in the crowd."

"Well?"

"I had another dream last night when I fell asleep in my chair after the street party"

"From what I can guess, I wouldn't describe it as 'falling asleep', Gabriel."

Gabriel managed a sheepish grin and said,

"Mary was in the dream, I'm sure of it, and once, she looked liked a much younger version of the girl in the crowd. It wasn't entirely a pleasant dream and …."

Naomi said nothing as Gabriel continued,

"And whatever else happened in the dream, Naomi, I know my sister is still alive – somewhere."

"Somewhere?"

"It seemed like I was in a different age – an age many years in the future and I was a child again, playing on the beach with some friends. The dream has become a bit muddled since last night but I can remember there was a little blond haired girl in it who was called Maggie. She spoke like Mary did."

"Well," said Naomi at last. "It seems to me that it's still just your mind playing tricks. Dreams mean nothing, Gabriel. They're just a random collection of events, all jumbled up over time and places. You can't read anything into them – they're not real, for goodness sake. The names you heard mean nothing. Maggie is probably just a name you've heard somewhere, just like you thought the girl in the crowd said Edward or Ed, maybe."

"Yes, my love, I know, but it seemed real to me. Maybe I'm going mad again."

"For pity's sake, don't say that, Gabriel. It was the drink to blame, started by a chance meeting with a strange girl that sparked off illogical memories. The only one round here who is mad is me – mad at you for getting drunk. You deserve to be feeling far worse than you appear this morning."

"Yes, I know."

"Well, I'm afraid it will take a lot from you for me to forgive you, Gabriel. You have made promises to me in the past about your drinking. Until I see those promises carried out, you are on trial, and please try to put thoughts about your sister out of your head. She may haunt you in your dreams but make sure they are not induced by whisky and maybe, just maybe, her memory will recede. Everyone else really believes she is dead after all this time without her being seen."

"Yes, Naomi, not a drop will pass my lips again."

Gabriel knew in his own mind that such a promise might be difficult to fulfil, given the strange thoughts that still plagued his mind, despite his wife's pragmatic explanation of his behaviour.

In another century, Christmas Eve had arrived with one little girl trying her utmost to be on her best behaviour. The previous day's shopping trip to Hamsden seemed to have been forgotten about as far as Maggie's mum was concerned, with breakfast that Saturday being a rushed affair after Gary had woken late. One or two too many glasses of wine the night before had taken its toll. Though it was Christmas Eve, he was still due at work at nine for the morning, which he always regarded as one of the busiest of the winter with interest in major surprise presents for loved ones at its highest. Pretending that he knew nothing about his daughter's antics of the day before, Gary found himself smiling and winking at Jenny on more than one occasion as he managed to down his black coffee and toast in less than half his normal time. He was just about to get up from the table when his daughter, who had hardly said a word till then – apart from the odd please or thank you – suddenly remarked,

"Mary is going to be good today, Daddy, or Father Christmas won't bring her any presents, will he."

Jenny's eyes rolled skywards but left it to Gary to reply.

"Yes, and I hope Maggie is going to be good as well. Otherwise she won't get anything either tomorrow, young lady."

"I'm always good – it's Mary that does bad things."

Jenny was about to protest her daughter's words but Gary put a finger to his lips.

"Really, Maggie? And please tell us how your dolly can do bad things when she can't move a muscle?"

"Because she makes me naughty, Daddy."

Jenny had had enough of her daughter's nonsense.

"Oh, don't be silly, Maggie, you're the one that's naughty, not Mary. Like your daddy says, she's just a doll. You have got to take responsibility when you're naughty."

Maggie frowned and asked,

"What's respon …, that word mean?"

"It means," said Gary, "that you can never blame someone else for the things you do."

"Oh."

Maggie was silent for a few seconds and Jenny was just about to suggest that it would not be such a bad idea if Mary was given away to another little girl when Maggie pre-empted her and said,

"P'raps if Mary was dead, I wouldn't be bad, Mummy."

This time, Jenny held a finger to her lips in case Gary made the obvious comment that her doll wasn't alive anyway.

"Do you want me to take her away from you, then?" asked Jenny.

"No, Mummy."

And then Maggie said something that seemed to be way beyond the intellectual capacity of a four-year-old and would leave both her parents open-mouthed.

"Anyway, it wouldn't do any good because when I was naughty yesterday, Mary wasn't with me. I left her in the car – remember, Mummy? It wouldn't matter where she was; she could still make me bad."

It took several seconds for Gary and Jenny to absorb their daughter's strange but clever analysis of her relationship with her favourite doll and the silence was only broken by Gary winking at Jenny and saying,

"Well, you'd better not say anything more, Maggie; before I inquire too deeply about yesterday's shopping trip. When you're naughty, you can blame nobody else but yourself, young lady, just like Mummy told you."

"Listen to your daddy, Maggie," said Jenny. "From now on, there will be no treats for you if you're naughty, especially when we're out shopping. Do you understand?"

"Yes, Mummy."

"And," said Jenny, "if needs be, and despite what you say, I shall take Mary away from you."

Before Maggie could say anything, Gary stood up and said,

"Right, I'm off to work. I just hope that Shelagh and Tom can cope till I get there – it's nearly nine already."

While Jenny followed her husband to the front door, Maggie made her way quietly and unnoticed to her bedroom. A few minutes later, when Jenny entered her daughter's room, she would discover her sobbing on her bed and clutching Mary to her chest. Although she couldn't be sure, it would seem to Jenny that Maggie had been talking to her doll before she had opened the door. Though it had been muffled, one particular sentence had registered in her mind, and it had frightened her. She would think about the words she'd heard for some time to come and they would cause her to cast some doubt on her daughter's sanity as well. Those words had sounded like:

'And you've got to be good from now on, Mary, or Mummy is going to kill you.'

Play-acting with her favourite doll was one thing, thought Jenny, but this was something different. What kind of reality was Maggie living in?

12
Maggie's Secret Friend

Just when Gabriel was in need of a hard day's fishing to ease the tension that was gripping his body, the weather took a turn for the worse that morning following on from his partial reconciliation with Naomi. He, Joshua and Amos had taken the *Richard Goodman* to the mouth of the Wentham where, in mid-summer, the mackerel were often abundant. Both Gabriel and his father had looked a little green at times but neither had disclosed how they were feeling after their excesses of the previous night. Though it had been rather breezy for late June, they had set off from Fenton in bright and warm sunshine. However, by the time they had reached the river mouth, dark clouds had started to approach from the east with worrying speed. The breeze became a moderate wind as they dropped anchor about a hundred yards off the jetty on the Canford side of the river. Gabriel's father looked at the darkening sky and shouted to Gabriel at the tiller,

"It looks bad, son. We ought to make for the jetty and rest up till she passes."

If his father had caught a glimpse of his son's face in close-up, he would have seen an unusually dark frown appear. Gabriel was clearly none too pleased at the prospect of inactivity, especially on the side of the river that brought back memories of times spent in the woods beyond, both in the real and his dream world. He called back over the strengthening wind,

"Oh, must we, Father – the anchor is down now. The weather doesn't look that bad."

Just then, and without warning, the fishing smack shuddered as a violent wave hit her broadside. Gabriel knew he had no choice and immediately set about weighing anchor.

"Take the tiller, Amos!" he shouted.

The old fisherman scampered nimbly across the deck and grabbed the swinging tiller. Joshua manned the mainsail and with the wind now on their starboard side, they sailed quickly across the estuary to the jetty. By the time they had safely moored the *Richard Goodman* in the lee of a large trawler, the rain was coming down in torrents, driven into their faces by the gale. After battening down all their gear, Gabriel sensed he knew how old Amos would want to occupy himself for the next hour or so until the storm abated. It was just after eleven.

"Come on, my lads," he shouted, as he climbed down onto the jetty. "I'm gonna' shelter in The Fisherman's Rest."

At first, Gabriel was hesitant and said,

"I think I'll stay with the boat."

"Don't be a fool, son," shouted his father, who clearly had every intention of joining Amos for some liquid refreshment. "You'll get drenched and there's nothing you can do here. She'll not come to any harm."

With some reluctance, Gabriel followed his father onto the landing stage and the three fishermen trudged up the beach to the shelter of the inn. His promise to Naomi was about to be put to the test. Amos was first to the bar.

"Right," he said to the landlord, "three glasses of your finest ale, if you please."

"Make that two," said Gabriel, hastily. "One of us should have a clear head for the return journey."

"Oh, come on," said Joshua. "One glass won't do you any harm – besides, if your throat is anything like mine after last night it will need lubricating again quickly. I'm as dry as the pipe of a blacksmith's bellows."

"No, Father," replied Gabriel. "I had enough for a long time last evening. I want nothing to drink."

"Oh, suit yourself then, son. I just hope we're not going to have to suffer your black face all lunchtime. Not got over last night, eh?"

"No, I'm fine – just tired, that's all."

As the three men pushed their way through the now busy inn to find a quiet table at the rear, Joshua whispered to his son,

"Still fretting over our Mary?"

"No," replied Gabriel. "Why do you ask?"

"Oh, Ma told me you'd called out her name in your sleep after I'd left you and gone to bed."

"Did I? I don't remember, Father."

Joshua put his fee arm round his son's shoulders and said,

"Don't worry, son, I miss her too."

Amos had found a table by now but only two chairs were available. Feeling a little giddy from the smoke-filled and oppressive atmosphere inside the inn, Gabriel appeared content to sit on the floor, below the descending curtain of smoke. He looked up at his father and said,

"You and Amos take the chairs. I have the wall for support."

After about an hour, by which time Amos and Joshua had consumed three glasses, the inn started to empty of its customers, most of whom had been only sheltering from the storm. To ease his limbs, stiff from sitting on the hard wooden floor, Gabriel made his way to the front of the inn to check the weather. He had good news when he returned to Joshua and Amos.

"The rain has stopped and the wind seems lighter. One or two boats are setting sail. We should make for the middle of the channel before the other boats get all the fish."

"Plenty of time, young Gabriel," said Amos with a wink.

"Yes, son," interjected Joshua. "I bet you it's only the small boats that are leaving."

"Yes, it seemed so," replied Gabriel. "How did you know?"

"Because it will be low tide in an hour and we won't get away from the jetty, so we can't set back until at least three this afternoon. Besides, Amos and I are going to have a portion of the landlord's game pie and some cheese to soak up our ale. Are you going to have the same, son?"

Gabriel glanced at the clock over the bar. It was just gone twelve-thirty. Nearly three hours to wait. He looked down at his father and smiled. He had known what he'd wanted to do almost as soon as they'd reached the mooring and now he had the perfect opportunity.

"Well, you can please yourselves but I'm going to get some air and go for a walk. I'll join you here later in plenty of time to go back."

"The woods?" asked Joshua, quietly.

"What?" said Gabriel.

"I said – are you going to go to the woods?"

"I don't know, Father – maybe."

Joshua smiled knowingly and said,

"Well, enjoy yourself and don't be fooled by any strange lights again. The sun is in the south now."

"Yes, Father, I won't."

As he made his way inland and headed for the woods, Gabriel thought about the light he'd seen before. He'd never really satisfied himself as to what it might have been and his father's casual mention of it had suddenly brought it back to mind. Then it struck him – it must have been the archway he'd seen in his dream. The sun must have been reflecting off its white marble-like surface. He stopped walking for a moment; the entrance to the woods lay just ahead. The day was warm again and he mopped his brow with his shirt sleeve. It still didn't seem to make sense. The portal had been in his dream, hadn't it? It couldn't be real and thus an explanation for the strange light?

He made quick progress through the woods. Somehow, he knew which way to go, as though he was following the same path as in his dream of the previous evening. Even the stifling nature of the woods seemed the same. The feeling of déjà vu was complete when, after about fifteen minutes, the semi-circle of elders once more came into view.

'*I knew you'd come back, Gabriel.*'

The voice echoed inside his head and Gabriel felt some relief. It was Mary, and she'd called him by his right name. He ran forward and joined the cliff path for the last few yards to the glade and, yes, it was there – the white portal, gleaming in the early afternoon sunshine. He stopped walking outside the entrance to the glade. He waited for Mary to say something, but there was no noise except for the rustle of the trees in the breeze. And then a thought came to him. Was he asleep and dreaming? Surely the strange archway could not be real? Had he fallen asleep in the inn without realising it? Surely not, as he still remembered the conversation with his father, but had that been part of his dream? He had to find out before he entered the semi-circle. Selecting a sharp twig from an overhanging branch, he took out his pocket knife and sharpened the short stick to a point. This might hurt, he thought, but it had to be done. Exposing his left forearm, he jabbed the stick into the flesh. It drew blood and a gasp of pain from his lips. He *was* awake.

'*What are you doing, dear brother?*'

Mary's voice seemed outside his head and very close. He entered the glade and turned to face the cliff edge.

'*You can't see me this time, Gabriel, but you know what to do, don't you.*'

"I'm not sure, Mary."

'*Oh, you know what to do, you silly boy. It's easy – you just have to trust me.*'

"Trust you – how?"

Mary did not reply. Gabriel tried hard to recall his dream. He walked round to the inward side of the portal and turned once more to face the cliff. What had happened next? He closed his eyes and waited. The trees seemed to sigh in the breeze but still Mary was silent. He had been on the beach at Fenton, hadn't he, but how had he got there? Then he remembered. All he had to do was walk through the portal and just keep on going over the edge. It had seemed easy in his dream, but this was reality and he knew you just didn't copy things that happened in dreams. He would kill himself; it was fifty feet or more to the shingle and rocks below. He could feel his heart beating faster. Mary was still silent. He tried to think logically. He had obeyed his sister's commands in his dream, so why not now? His remembered that his dream had seemed real enough at the time and yet he still had plucked up the courage to walk through the portal and over the edge. He closed his eyes again and offered up a silent prayer for God's protection. He walked forward and even as he did so he couldn't believe the stupidity of what he was about to do. Ignoring any thoughts for his safety, he reached the cliff edge, closed his eyes once more, and stepped into space.

'*Hurrah! Gabriel's coming!*'

He felt nothing – no sensation of falling, just warmth and a light-headedness. He tried to open his eyes but they seemed glued tightly shut.

'*Ooh, you're bleeding, Ed! Does it hurt?*'

He felt his left arm throbbing with pain. It was Mary's voice.

'*Mummy will have a plaster in her bag.*'

At last, his senses started to return; he could hear the sea and the waves breaking on the shore. His eyes opened once more. He was sitting on the sand, facing the sea. He glanced behind him. It was like his dream; Fenton had changed. It seemed years in the future. The little girl was sitting beside him. She had blond hair and looked to be about six. Her legs were bare. What was a plaster? What *was* the girl's name? His mind was in turmoil. He spoke almost automatically.

"No, it's fine, Mary," he said.

"Mary's gone, silly. I'm six now and I don't have a doll anymore. My name's Maggie, Ed – don't call me Mary. She was naughty."

"Oh, I'm sorry, Maggie, and how old am I, then?"

"Oh you are stupid, Ed – you're dead. Mummy says you went away before I was born."

Initially, Gabriel made no comment about his new name as he tried to make sense of his new situation. Where was the boy from his dream? After a few seconds of thought, he knew he had to question the girl.

"So, if I'm dead, how come you can see me and I can see you?"

"That's easy, silly – you're a ghost. I've seen you lots of times."

"Where?"

"Here, on the beach. Minor saw you once, but he doesn't remember."

"Has anyone else seen me?"

"No, of course not."

"Have you told your parents about me?"

"Yes, but they think I'm mad. I have to see a doctor next week, but I'm going to tell him about you. He'll believe me."

"Who is Minor?"

"Oh, Ed, you are stupid. Minor was your best friend when you were alive. Mummy told me. He lives on a farm and they have lots of cows – black and white ones."

"How old do I look now – as a ghost, I mean?"

"I don't know – older than me, maybe about sixteen. My friend Camilla Parkinson has a brother and he's sixteen. You look about his age. Mummy says you went away when you were eight."

"How do you know I'm your brother?"

Gabriel thought he had caught the little girl out but after a pause, she replied,

"I just know, Ed, and anyway, you look like the boy in the photos that Mummy and Daddy have got at home."

"What are pho-tos?"

Gabriel pronounced the word slowly.

"Pictures, silly."

"Oh," said Gabriel. This was difficult.

"Where is your home?"

"Acacia Avenue."

"Where's that?"

"Up the town and past the railway station."

"What town?"

"Oh, you are a silly ghost – why Fenton-on-Sea, of course."

"Ah," said Gabriel, wistfully. "And what is your surname, little girl."

"My name's Maggie and I'm not little."

She paused and looked into Gabriel's eyes.

"What's a surname?"

"Your last name, like mine is Thomas."

"Thomas?"

"Yes, I'm called Gabriel Thomas in my other world."

Gabriel was finally coming to terms with his strange situation and he was consequently determined to preserve his sanity and identity at all costs. Maggie frowned deeply.

"Do ghosts go to another world, then, and are called something else?"

"Apparently – yes, Maggie. So, tell me, what is your last name?"

"Compton-Jones, but only my teacher, Miss Carter, calls me Maggie Compton-Jones. I don't like it. The other children call me names."

"What does your brother look like in the pictures?"

"Like you, silly – I told you."

"And what do I look like?"

Maggie looked puzzled by the conundrum. Gabriel tried to make it simpler.

"What colour hair do I have?"

"Don't you know, Ed?"

"No."

"Black."

Well that's one good thing, thought Gabriel.

"What are you parents' names, Maggie?"

"Jenny and Gary, but I'm not allowed to call them that."

"I see."

"Anyway," said Maggie, suddenly, "I've got to go now; Mummy will be worried."

"Where is Mummy?"

"Over there on the promenade. She's on that seat talking to Mrs Thompson."

Gabriel glanced at the promenade. He could just make out two women on a seat in the distance.

"Won't she ask you who you've been talking to on the beach?"

"No, silly, she can't see you – you're a ghost. Anyway, I'll just say I've been talking to my invisible friend. They know I have one. I used to call him Ed, after you, but I shall call him Gabriel from now on, after your new name. I hope you'll come again, Gabriel. I often sit down by the water when Mummy brings me down here."

"Yes, I hope so, too, Maggie."

Maggie stood up and as she turned to go, Gabriel had one last question he had to ask.

"What year is it, Maggie?"

"1985, silly – bye!"

"Goodbye, Maggie."

After the little girl had gone to rejoin her mother, Gabriel didn't move for quite some time. A few odd looking people walked by but he was clearly invisible as one young man seemed to pass right through him. None of what had happened seemed to make any sense to him. Question after question ran through his head. The little girl called herself Maggie but had sounded just like his sister, Mary. What had she meant by saying, '*Mary was naughty*'? Was she referring only to her doll which she didn't have anymore? Why had she mistaken him for her dead brother? Was it just a coincidence that he looked like the boy in the pictures or was there another reason? How could he have two identities? How could he possibly be in the future, and nearly ninety years at that, if the girl was to be believed? He wanted to go up the beach and explore the town, because, looking behind him, Fenton seemed to have doubled in size. Could he find his old house at South Beach Terrace or his and Naomi's new one on the cliff top? He closed his eyes and tried to think straight. He had to be in a dream but when had it started? Did he fall asleep at the glade? Where was his real sister? What was reality and what was just a dream? He couldn't tell which was which. His head began to throb from the previous evening's drinking. He was tired. It was all too much for him. He lay back on the sand. His eyes closed in sleep – his lips felt wet and he had a strange sensation that Maggie was kissing him.

'Now you know what it's like, Gabriel. Now you know how it feels to be mad. I will show you more when you come next time. I will turn you into someone else. Now you had better get back to Father and Amos. They will be waiting for you.'

Mary's voice was whispering in his ear. Or *was* it Maggie who had come back? He opened his eyes. There were trees overhead. He was back at the glade of elders. The white portal had gone and he was sitting on the ground. Gabriel jumped up with a start. He looked at his left forearm. There was no mark. It had to have been a dream, but he hadn't been to sleep; he was sure of that. He was certain he'd been awake for the whole time. It had been a waking dream. He shuddered as his sister's words echoed in his head. '*Now you know how it feels to be mad*'. It had been a demonstration of a strange and unknown power and it scared him. He turned and ran from the glade. How long had he been? Ignoring the brambles and branches that scratched his face, he charged through the woods, only slowing to a walk when he at last emerged into the bright sunlight. From the position of the sun, he judged it still to be early afternoon. He mouthed his thanks heavenwards.

Five minutes later, the landing stage came into view. They were at the boat. He could see them in the distance. He waved and shouted,

"Wait for me! I'm coming!"

His father waved back. Everything seemed normal. He slowed his pace as he approached the jetty. Fifty yards to go and Amos shouted to him,

"Good timing, lad. It's three o'clock by my watch."

Gabriel breathed a sigh of relief as he slowed right down to a nonchalant saunter.

"Are you alright, son?"

His father looked at him with a puzzled and worried face.

"You've got yourself in a right mess by the look of it. Where did you go? You should always stick to the paths. Those woods can be like a jungle in summer."

"Looks like he's been to hell and back, Joshua," said Amos, grinning from ear to ear."

"Did you find anything, son?" said Joshua, more sympathetically.

Gabriel smiled, ruefully.

"No, Father, I got lost. I truly don't know where I've been. I found no trace of Mary. I think you and Ma must be right – she is gone."

"Well, at least you're back safe and sound. I suggest we abandon any attempts to fish and make our way straight back to the South Quay. I think we've all had enough for one day. Ma'll get you cleaned up before you go back to Naomi. She's bound to have some of your old clothes you can change into, son."

"Yes, Father, I'm tired and want to go home."

Gabriel had been away for the best part of three hours on a fruitless search that had led him into another world – another world that his real sister had led him to. Two questions would weigh him down on the sail home. First, why did Mary want him to see the other world and second, why did they each seem to have two distinct and separate identities which existed in different worlds nearly a century apart, apparently linked only by a brother-sister relationship? The situation was becoming worse by the day, as Gabriel found he was unable even to rely on the reality of his waking hours to preserve his sanity. Nightmares were bad enough when you were asleep but waking ones were far worse, making him question reality itself.

13

A Bloody Nose and a Strange Young Man

Maggie Compton-Jones didn't go to school on a Wednesday; indeed, she didn't go to school on a Thursday or a Friday either. When she did attend an educational establishment, on two days out of five, it was not the kind to be associated with a normal six-year-old. Jenny and Gary had known for nearly a year that their only daughter was definitely not normal. Her behaviour in public had got far worse than the events just before Christmas eighteen months previously. They had only been a precursor of many extraordinary battles between Maggie and her long-suffering parents. Many a shopkeeper had to clear up after a visit from Maggie and her mother; the spillages ranging from displays pushed over to more serious assaults with their own goods. Any loose packaging was always a prime target for her busy fingers and the contents, whether liquid or solid, occasionally ended up all over the bewildered shopkeeper. By the previous spring, Maggie and Jenny had been barred from most shops in Fenton-on-Sea and Hamsden as well. Maggie's 'mood swings', as Gary had once described his daughter's ability to change from a raging monster to a charming penitent little girl, were quickly diagnosed by their local GP, Dr Rees, as a serious mental condition that could not just be explained by the normal problems associated with growing up. The temper tantrums had got so bad that Dr Rees eventually had to conclude that Maggie had some kind of 'disruptive disorder', the precise medical name and details of which were way beyond his expertise. She was referred to a consultant psychiatrist at the Hamsden County Hospital on June the 25th, the previous summer, for testing and analysis of her condition. She was just five years old.

Though the psychiatrist prescribed certain drugs to control Maggie's disorder, he did warn her parents that her condition might well get worse and that there were definite signs of a psychotic nature in her behaviour. In short, she had a mental problem that would require careful and individual monitoring. He also recorded that normal primary school would not be beneficial for Maggie or, indeed, the other pupils. Despite the expense, Jenny and Gary managed to obtain a place for her at Castle Hill Special School in Hamsden where she started as a day pupil on September the 7th, 1984. They could afford only two days at the privately run school for children with serious mental problems, known locally, by other children in the area, as the 'nuthouse'. Jenny had already previously given up her part-time job at the hairdressing salon, *Curls and Twirls*, in Hamsden, after her parents had refused to babysit their granddaughter. Now, her role became one of a full-time unpaid carer for her sad daughter for the five days when she was not attending the special school. Permanent residency at Castle Hill was not out of the question as 1984 rolled into 1985. Jenny and Gary's life had become dominated by their daughter's mental condition. By the spring, it was getting too much for them to bear by themselves. They needed help and a chance remark from Ann Compton, Jenny's mother, opened up that possibility. She said that she thought Brenda Thompson, who she knew from St Andrew's Church, had been a qualified mental health nurse before she took early retirement and might well be able to offer some assistance. So, from the beginning of June, Mrs Thompson, one-time nurse and now local busybody, was employed at minimal expense to relieve Jenny for a couple of hours on the three weekdays when Maggie was not in school. Jenny and Gary still felt able to cope with their daughter at weekends and other times, provided, of course, they kept her at home where her condition seemed to be controllable; her psychotic and disruptive behaviour often being replaced by a silent depressive state spent sitting in her bedroom.

Thus it was on Wednesday, June the 23rd that Jenny and Mrs Thompson happened to be sharing a promenade bench in the warm afternoon sunshine. After doing her shopping, Maggie's mother had joined her helper who had taken her daughter for what was becoming a regular visit to the beach. Brenda Thompson had discovered, quite by chance, that Maggie seemed to love nothing better that just sitting on the sands in silent contemplation while her guardian watched from a suitably close vantage point a few yards away.

"She seems to be talking to herself again, Jennifer," remarked Brenda Thompson, after they had watched Maggie for about ten minutes or so."

"Yes," replied Jenny. "She has a special friend she talks to after we threw her doll, Mary, away. She pretends it's her dead brother, Ed."

"But she never knew him, Jenny."

"I know, but Gary and I must have talked so much about him that she thinks she did. Dr Ableson at Hamsden County Hospital says it's all part of her condition – make-believe and so on, you know. He says she has probably done it since she first learned to communicate. I just wish we'd known then. We used to think that she was hiding behind her doll whenever she was naughty and was blaming her for it, but Dr Ableson says she probably genuinely believed that Mary was a real person and was responsible for her own bad behaviour. It's just so sad, Brenda. I sometimes wish we hadn't got rid of Mary."

"Couldn't you buy her another doll to replace it?"

"We tried that as soon as we discovered the full extent of her condition but she went completely ballistic and tried to flush it down the loo. It's all part of the psychosis which can be so frightening if you're not prepared for it.

"I know," said Brenda Thompson, quietly, as if she had already experienced such an event."

Jenny glanced down the beach. Her daughter was waving at the sea.

"Ah," said Jenny. "Here she comes. She's had enough of talking to Ed by the looks of it."

"I'll walk home with you, if I may, Jenny," said Brenda.

"That would be nice – we always go up Brook Lane and avoid the town. It's for the best. She doesn't get so distracted that way."

"Fine."

Maggie walked slowly up to her mother and said,

"He's called Gabriel now, Mummy."

"Who is, love?"

"Ed, of course, you silly thing, and he's older now. He didn't recognise me, Mum. I can't think why – he's seen me before."

"Has he, dear?" said Jenny, winking at Brenda Thompson. They both knew they had to humour her if they were to avoid a confrontation.

"Yes, and he's last name is Thomas, he says, not Compton-Jones."

"Oh," said Brenda Thompson. "I wonder why that is, dear."

"Because he's a ghost, silly. Ghosts don't live here and they change their names when they move. Gabriel told me. Do you believe in ghosts, Mrs Thompson?"

And then the charade ended as Brenda Thompson was too honest with her reply.

"No, dear, I don't – there are no such things."

Jenny tried to grab her daughter as she knew that Brenda had said the wrong thing but she was a second too late as her daughter lashed out with a balled fist and struck Brenda Thompson squarely on the nose, instantly drawing a gush of blood. Maggie screamed at the top of her voice,

"You stupid old woman! I hate you, and so does Gabriel! I'm going to find him and I'll show you."

Mrs Thompson's spectacles flew off her nose and landed with a clatter on the concrete promenade. Her mouth popped open with shock as a stream of blood continued to curl down her chin.

"Oh, my God," screamed Jenny, as she made a second lunge for her daughter but Maggie was too quick and she tried to aim a second punch at her mother. The force of the swing nearly took her off her feet, so ferocious was the anger contained within its momentum. Having missed her target, Maggie regained her balance and ran, shouting and screaming, down the beach to the sea.

"Gabriel! Gabriel! Help me!"

Jenny was torn between offering some emergency medical treatment to Brenda Thompson and retrieving her daughter, who seemed bound on a blind headlong dash for the water. Shaking her head, her friend mumbled incoherently and waved Jenny away. It was enough to tip the balance in favour of rescuing her daughter from a dip in the North Sea.

"Maggie!" she shouted. "Come back here at once!"

Jenny had long ago abandoned adding something like, '*you naughty girl*' to any of her admonitions as it always seemed to inflame her daughter's anger even more. Teachers at Castle Hill had told her that commands had to be clear and simple and should involve neither an element of compromise nor be judgemental. No comment should be made on whether her actions were right or wrong; good and evil were not concepts that Maggie readily understood.

At that moment, Maggie seemed to have no concept that the sea would form a natural barrier to her progress and she ploughed straight into it, the water soon reaching up beyond her waist. Jenny was only a few yards behind her daughter when suddenly Maggie dived forward, flinging herself face down with outstretched arms into the surf. Her little body disappeared beneath the rolling waves. Jenny screamed.

"Maggie! Don't drown!"

She jumped into the water, her legs kicking upwards and outwards to aid her forward motion. She quickly reached the spot where she had last seen her daughter, took a deep gulp of air and dived beneath the surface. Her right arm made quick contact with one of her daughter's legs and she pulled the small limb towards her. With the rest of Maggie's body following, Jenny was able to lift her daughter clear of the water and pull her to safety. She laid her carefully on the beach and knew at once that Maggie's life was in danger when the expected resistance to her rescue had not materialised. Jenny bent down and looked at her apparently lifeless body. Oh, where was Gary? He would know what to do. A gruff voice beside her suddenly said,

"Here, my lady, let me do it – I'm used to saving folk who are drowning."

A tall swarthy young man bent over Maggie's face and parted her lips. He blew a sharp burst of air into her mouth, simultaneously pressing hard on her chest. The operation was repeated twice more till, to Jenny's great relief, a small fountain of sea water gushed from her daughter's mouth.

"Oh, thank God," moaned Jenny.

"No, just be thankful that I'm a fisherman," said the black haired young man.

"Oh, how can I ever repay you?" said Jenny.

"No need, madam. It was lucky I was just passing through."

Maggie's eyes had fluttered open and she tried to say something. The young man stood up and made way for Jenny who put a finger to her daughter's lips.

"Shh, Maggie. You're safe now."

The anger seemed to have gone and Maggie sat up. She looked to one side and smiled sweetly. Jenny held her hand and said,

"Yes, you must thank this young man. He has just saved your life."

Maggie looked at her mother but said nothing. Jenny turned to the young man and said,

"She has not been well, I'm afraid, so I apologise that she feels unable to thank you."

Her words had fallen on deaf ears as the handsome young stranger had disappeared. Jenny jumped up and looked all around her but he was nowhere to be seen. He had vanished into thin air. Though it would never really register with Jenny, her daughter stood up and whispered,

"There you are – I told you so. I told you he was here."

An hour later, at Fenton Cottage Hospital, Maggie seemed calmer – the paramedic had commented to Jenny how well-behaved her little girl had been in the ambulance, which had been quickly summoned by another passer-by. Mrs Thompson, whose nose had been patched up by the same paramedic who'd attended to Maggie, had watched the whole scene unfold from her position on the promenade. She had stormed off and walked home unaided, muttering that Jenny had better find someone else to help her with her daughter. Later, she would deny having made the remark, putting it down to shock. When, the following day, Jenny told her about the young man who had performed the mouth-to-mouth, she would vehemently deny seeing any such man. Jenny even began to doubt her own sanity over the issue, let alone her daughter's. Though she told several people, the paramedics included, about her daughter's lifesaver, no one ever came forward to acknowledge their vital deed. The image of the tall, black haired young man, who had been wearing clothes that Jenny would later describe as curiously old-fashioned, would play on her mind for some time to come. She was sure there had been no one near her daughter when she had made her frightening dash for the sea.

By chance, while Maggie was being checked over and equipped with some dry clothes, Jenny's local GP, Dr Rees, popped into the out-patient's department. He seemed to have heard from the staff in casualty about Maggie's narrow escape from drowning. Seeing Jenny sitting in a corner waiting for Maggie to emerge, he came over and sat beside her.

"Seems like Maggie's been a very lucky girl. How on earth did she come to be in the water? Was it one of her attacks?"

"Yes, Doctor," said a tearful Jenny. "She punched Mrs Thompson in the nose and attempted to do the same to me. Then she just ran into the sea where she flung herself under the water. It was horrible, Dr Rees."

"I can imagine. What a shame for poor old Brenda Thompson. It couldn't have happened to a nicer person, eh?"

The doctor winked at Jenny. She tried to raise a smile at his telling remark. Brenda Thompson had a reputation in Fenton of spreading gossip and the good doctor had experienced her wagging tongue on more than one occasion when it had concerned confidential information about his patients. He could never fathom out how she got hold of the privileged information in the first place.

"Well, it's a good thing she's got her monthly check-up at the County Hospital next week. I understand they're going to do a brain scan this time."

"Are they?" asked Jenny, nervously.

"Yes, but try not to worry too much, it has to be done in such cases."

"Oh."

"You do know that Maggie's prognosis is not good, don't you?"

"Yes, I suppose so."

"And you are prepared for the worst, aren't you?"

"The worst?"

"She might have to be taken into full residential care. You and your husband will find it increasingly difficult to cope with her."

Jenny was quiet. She and Gary had known of the possibility for a while but had tried to get on with their lives and put it to the back of their minds. After a few seconds, she asked,

"Where?"

"Well, it could be one of several places, but probably Castle Hill to begin with – on a trial period."

"Won't that cost?"

"Probably not, Jenny, if the consultant psychiatrist recommends it. The county has funds for such cases. Does she like it there when she goes at the moment?"

"Yes, I think so. She's always much better behaved on a Wednesday after she's been on a Tuesday."

"Well, that's a good sign. The school will be asked for their opinion on the suitability of full-time care for her there."

Dr Rees looked up. A nurse was escorting Maggie back to her mother after her check-up.

"Anyway here she is now. I'd better leave you to take her home. I think an ambulance has been summoned. I'll be in touch after next week."

Maggie was quiet and submissive in the ambulance and went straight up to her bedroom without saying a word to Jenny or Gary who had arrived home early from work after his wife's call from the hospital. Jenny clung to her husband for a good five minutes as she sobbed into his neck. The situation with her daughter had taken a step for the worse. The two anxious parents spent a long evening talking about the future and the impending psychiatric tests. By the time they both went to bed later that night, they had resigned themselves to the worst, whatever that should mean for their daughter. Maggie did not leave her room and she ate or drank nothing that was offered to her. Jenny and Gary lost count of the times that they popped their heads round her bedroom door, only to find her either asleep or sitting on her bed silently rocking backwards and forwards with her arms clasped round her knees. At no time did she show any sign of noticing that they had entered her room to check on her.

14
Tests

Maggie remained in a quiet and somewhat depressed state of mind almost until the following Tuesday, the day of her appointment at Hamsden County Hospital with consultant psychiatrist Dr Ableson. Spending much of the time in her bedroom and only reluctantly eating and drinking minimal amounts of liquid and food, her parents had more time than usual to openly discuss their daughter's condition. It was soon clear that each of them had different views on what the future should hold for their only daughter. Sunday lunchtime brought the argument that had been brewing silently. Maggie had put in a brief appearance for some of her favourite roast beef dinner and had just retired to her room. Jenny began to open up her heart.

"You know, Gary, I don't want Maggie to be institutionalised, don't you?"

"Mm, I suppose so, love, but we have to do what's best for her."

"What's best for her is to stay at home with me and, if we can afford it, send her to Castle Hill for an extra day or two as a day pupil. Could we afford it?"

"No," replied Gary. "Only if you were able to work. Second-hand cars aren't selling at the moment. Everyone seems to be tightening their belts with the downturn in the economy. Besides, they would only take her on advice from the consultant psychiatrist and if he recommends that she goes resident then we wouldn't have the choice."

Jenny's frustration began to come to the surface and she said,

"It's easy for you just to go along with the doctors. It takes away the responsibility for you."

"That's not fair, Jenny, I'm as concerned as you are over Maggie and I just think we should follow the professional advice. They know best, after all."

"Well it wouldn't be you that would have to look after her if she did stay at home."

"Oh, come on, love, I have to work so we can live. You're talking nonsense now. I think next week's appointment is getting to you and you need to think about the consequences more logically. You know how you exaggerate situations sometimes. You'll be alright after the tests."

"Don't you patronise me, Gary Jones – I know what's best for our daughter even if you want to abdicate your responsibilities. Brenda and I can cope with her."

"Huh? Like you did last Wednesday when she nearly drowned? Don't be silly, dear. If it hadn't been for this strange boy you keep talking about, she wouldn't be with us anymore."

Jenny glared at her husband, her voice getting louder and more agitated by the minute.

"Yeah? You'd like that, wouldn't you?"

"No, of course I wouldn't. I just want what's best for Maggie and you would do well to remember that, Jen. It's not what you or I want – that's selfish, and you should know that. Her happiness and quality of life are the most important things as well as the professional care that we can't give her."

"Well, I think she's happy here."

"Oh yeah? So how come she's been in her bedroom almost permanently for the past four days. She might as well be in a locked room at the school. She obviously doesn't need our company, does she?"

"She came and had some dinner with us, didn't she?"

"Only because you went up four times and shouted at her as though you were a sergeant major in the army or something. That's no way to deal with her."

"That just shows how much you know, Gary. If you'd listened properly to what Dr Ableson told us, you'd know that if you want to get Maggie to do something you have to issue clear and unequivocal commands but, of course, I forgot, you missed her last two appointments."

"You know that was unavoidable; I had customers to see and I would have lost sales."

"Yeah, your job is more important than your daughter's well-being."

For the first time, Gary raised his voce in anger.

"Oh, don't be stupid. If I don't sell cars, then we don't live; Maggie included!"

"Don't you call me stupid, Gary Jones!" shouted Jenny, loudly.

"Calm down, Jenny, for goodness sake or Maggie will hear you."

"*It's alright, Daddy, Gabriel and I know you don't want us.*"

Gary froze. How much of their 'conversation' had his daughter heard? Jenny looked up to see Maggie standing in the dining room doorway. She jumped up to comfort her.

"There, there, Maggie, it's alright, love. Daddy and I were just talking."

"Am I going away, then, Mummy?"

"No," said Jenny, "you're not going away."

Rather than seeming pleased at her mother's reassurance, Maggie's face dropped and she said,

"Oh – Gabriel says it's nicer where he lives. I want to go there, too."

Without saying another word, she squirmed out of Jenny's hug and walked calmly out of the room. After a moment or two, her parents heard the dull thud as her bedroom door closed once more. Silence descended on the dining room. The argument had been brought to an abrupt halt by Maggie's strange request. After what seemed an age, Gary broke the silence.

"Who is Gabriel, Jen?"

"Oh, didn't I tell you? It's her new name for her special friend – the one she used to call Ed, after her brother."

"Where did she get the name Gabriel from? It's not exactly a common name."

"I have no idea; I don't know how her mind works. Maybe someone at Castle Hill is called Gabriel."

"And what did she mean by *'where Gabriel lives'*? asked Gary.

"I don't know that either, or why it should be nicer. It's all in her mind, Gary."

"Well, maybe the tests next this week will throw some light on the workings of her brain. And, Jenny …."

"Yes?"

"I'm sorry I shouted and seem to you to be unconcerned. I'm as worried about the future as you are, but sometimes I feel more comfortable in putting my trust in what the professionals say."

Jenny said nothing and a few tears started to roll down her cheeks. She knew, deep down, that her husband was right. Her trepidation at the forthcoming visit to Hamsden County Hospital was due mostly to her silent acceptance that Gary's view on the future for their daughter would indeed come to pass.

Dr Sam Ableson's appearance was in complete contrast to that of the sober, grey-suited Dr Rees who had been a local GP in Fenton-on-Sea for over thirty years; long enough to have tended to all the normal childhood diseases of both Maggie's parents. Samuel Ableson was tall and lanky and was accustomed to wear an open-necked check shirt with a pair of denim jeans. His casual working attire said much about the ten years he had spent in the States both for his doctorate in psychiatry and while an intern at the famous Pilgrim's Children's Hospital in Boston as one of seven junior psychiatrists. He was one of only two at Hansden County and was widely regarded as one of the top men in his field. Unlike Dr Rees' short grey hair, Dr Ableson's was long, fair and tied in a small pigtail at the back. He was of comparable age to Jenny and Gary, being still just in his thirties. His pop star image did much to calm his young patient's anxieties, if not totally providing confidence in his abilities for their parents. Jenny and Gary liked him, both for his open honesty and his informality. Jenny always listened to him intently, almost in awe of his acquired transatlantic accent. He welcomed Maggie and her parents in his bright office on the top floor of the Spencer Wing a little after two on the afternoon of Tuesday, June the 29th. While a young female assistant looked after Maggie in a play area adjacent to the main suite of rooms, Sam Ableson sat at his desk with her file open before him.

"Well, how has she been?"

Jenny looked at Gary, unsure how to reply or what the psychiatrist knew. Dr Ableson sensed their awkwardness.

"I have heard, you know. Dr Rees sent a detailed report of Maggie's accident. I meant for the rest of the time."

"About the same, I suppose," said Jenny. "But …."

"But she's a lot quieter sometimes, eh? Seems to be depressed?" interrupted the psychiatrist.

"Yes," said Gary. "But how did you know? She's only really been like that since last Wednesday after she attempted to drown herself."

"It's a natural progression," drawled Sam Ableson. "Her behaviour has started to become one of extremes – extremely disruptive and frightening one minute and passively depressed the next. It's typical of her condition – they are classic symptoms at this stage."

"This stage?" queried Jenny.

"Yes, there will be further developments. Her life now is going to be one of plateaus."

"I don't follow," said Jenny.

"What I mean by that is that for a while now her behaviour has been reasonably constant. For the last two months or so up until last Wednesday, she was on a plateau. Now she has moved to the next one. No one can tell how long she will remain on each plateau."

"And these plateaus – her condition worsens as she moves from one to the next?" asked Gary, nervously.

"Not necessarily. Her behaviour will just take on a different form each time. Her condition may or may not worsen, as you put it. This time, from your point of view, it has worsened, but it may be a different story from how she sees it. From what I can see, she has reached another plateau where she may be in this depressive state for some time. Such a state can be as worrying and scary as one that is extremely violent. In some cases, when children become violent and undergo extreme behavioural changes, they are often happier as a result. Remember, you must try to think of Maggie's emotions and not your own."

Gary looked at Jenny and smiled.

"So what are the tests for today?" said Jenny.

"I was coming to that," replied the psychiatrist. "All in good time. I just wanted you to be aware that you must try to understand things from your daughter's point of view. You know by now that she is never going to get better and all we can do is try to control her condition at each stage, using whatever technique is best for her. So far, a balanced combination of special education and home care has been enough. The latest incident suggests we might need more careful monitoring and professional care. You do understand what I'm saying, don't you?"

"You mean she might have to be resident at Castle Hill?" said Jenny.

"Maybe – but there are other institutions that might be more appropriate."

Sam Ableson paused before continuing.

"But, hey, let's not jump to conclusions before we've got all the data."

He leant back in his chair and addressed his female assistant.

"Sally, take Maggie down to the assessment room, please."

Maggie seemed unconcerned at this announcement and allowed Sally to take her hand. They made for the door. Maggie said nothing.

"Shall I go with her?" asked Jenny.

"No need, I think. She seems just fine right now. Best not to upset her equilibrium – it may frighten her, Jenny," replied Dr Ableson.

"O.K., Dr Ableson," said Jenny. "How long will she be?"

"About an hour, all being well. You can wait here or there's a small café down the corridor. I'll come and find you when we're done."

"We'll stay here, won't we, Gary."

"Yeah, no problem," said the psychiatrist. "There are plenty of magazines and books over in the corner and I'll see you later. And please don't worry – she's in safe hands."

After Dr Ableson had gone, Jenny and Gary sat reading for a while, neither saying much to the other. Most of what the psychiatrist had said had made sense but one sentence, in particular, was playing on both their minds. They had both guessed what the *'other institutions'* might include.

Dr Ableson returned in less than forty minutes. Maggie was not with him. He was carrying a new and much larger folder than the one Jenny and Gary had seen earlier containing their daughter's notes. He walked to one side of the room and flicked a switch that lit up a small X-ray type observation screen.

"You'd better come and see these," he said. Jenny and Gary got up from their chairs and prepared themselves to look at the screen.

"These are some images of Maggie's brain."

Jenny reached for her husband's hand. The news did not sound good. The first transparency of their daughter's scan was in place.

"You will see that the left side of the brain has dark patches," Sam Ableson said, calmly and without emotion. It was like he was reading out a railway timetable. "Those are areas where the brain has deteriorated badly. They represent substantial gaps where the brain has receded and the spaces are now filled with fluid."

He switched transparencies.

"This one is taken from the side. The erosion in brain tissue is both linear and vertical."

He reached for a third negative. Jenny held up her hand and said,

"No more, Dr Ableson. I have heard enough."

She flopped into the chair in front of the psychiatrist's desk. Gary shook his head and said,

"Thank you, Dr Ableson – you must tell us what it all means."

"Of course."

The psychiatrist returned to his chair. He clasped his hands behind his head.

"You'd better sit down, too, Gary."

"I'd prefer to stand."

"As you wish."

Dr Ableson looked at Jenny.

"The prognosis is not good, I'm afraid. In fact, it is quite remarkable that Maggie is able to function as she does. Fortunately, at the moment, the damaged parts of her brain are not affecting her ability to carry out normal physical movement or even the ability to think and talk properly. The only outward sign of the brain's malfunction is her extreme passiveness which presents itself as the depressive state you have seen recently."

Jenny seemed to take the news rather better than Dr Ableson had thought she would.

"Please go on," she said quietly when the psychiatrist seemed to pause for a moment or two, expecting her to protest his analysis. "What does it mean?"

"Well, I'm afraid her time on the present plateau is likely to be brief."

"And what will the next one involve?" said Gary.

"I can't give you a complete answer to that," replied Sam Ableson. "All I do know is that she may start to lose some physical abilities which would prevent her from carrying out some natural functions of her body."

"Will she become violent again," asked Jenny.

"It's possible. When the brain gets damaged like this the various messages that are sent to various parts of the body get confused and become more random in nature. It's impossible to say what will happen, but …."

Jenny and Gary waited for the psychiatrist to continue.

"But I must advise constant and professional monitoring. Do you understand what I'm saying?"

"Ye-es," stammered Jenny. "I think so. She will have to go into care."

"Yes, I'm afraid she is about to become too much for you and Gary to cope with."

"Where?" asked Gary.

"Well, initially I think she can go to Castle Hill as a boarder and we will monitor the situation over the next month."

Jenny looked on the verge of breaking down. Her lower jaw quivered as she asked,

"Whe-en will she go?"

"It would be best she goes today, Jenny. I talked to her while she was having her scan and she did not seem upset when I mentioned the prospect of going to the school this afternoon. In fact she seemed quite pleased as long as someone she knew was going to be there."

"Who?" said Gary.

"Someone called Gabriel. I'm afraid I said he would be there even though I have no idea who he is. Do you?"

"Yes," replied Jenny. "He's her special imaginary friend."

"Imaginary?"

"Yes, she invented him recently. She used to call him Ed after our dead son. You know about that, don't you?"

"Yes, it's in my notes. So this Gabriel is a make-believe character?"

"Yes."

"Well, that explains a lot. This Gabriel is not make-believe to Maggie, you know. He is as real to her as you or I – in fact he will be more of a reality to her than most everyday situations she comes across.

In her world – and it is a different world from ours – she may well have a whole range of make-believe people that form her circle of friends. In short, we have already lost her to a new kind of reality, hence her subdued attitude. She will probably talk quite freely and lucidly about Gabriel and her other friends for some time if you prompt her. She doesn't relate to or understand our world anymore. If you try to bring her back to our reality by admonishing her or shouting at her then that's when she could become violent."

"So she's happy, then?" said Gary.

"Yes, in her own way."

Finally, Jenny broke down in tears and clung to Gary for comfort. She tried to talk between sobs.

"So, that's it – I-I've lost her for good."

Dr Ableson did not reply but offered instead a sympathetic smile. They would not see Maggie again that afternoon as her new life, no matter how temporary, had begun. When, the following afternoon, they went to visit her in her own room at Castle Hill Special School and Care Home, their daughter gave them no indication that she wanted to talk to them or, indeed, even recognised them. She was in a new world.

15

A Waking Nightmare

Ever since his previous visit to another century, Gabriel was convinced in his own mind that the little girl, Maggie, was a reincarnation of his sister, Mary. Although he didn't really understand anything of the details of a process that he'd only read about in books, it all seemed to make some kind of sense to him. Unlike Naomi, his upbringing had not been a strictly religious one and his mind had always been open to new ideas, and the suggestion that Mary was living in a different body nearly a hundred years in the future appealed to him. Her 'escape' from Canford Asylum had not only been a physical one, he concluded, but a spiritual one as well. Over the latter days of the summer of 1897, it gave him some comfort that there would be no further point in trying to seek Mary out in the physical sense. Perhaps, therefore, there was no need to visit the woods again with its strange glade.

So it was that Gabriel took to sitting on the beach at Fenton whenever he could and at times during the day when it would not raise any suspicions as to his motive for doing so. At home, Naomi had noticed that he seemed to be calmer with regard to his sleeping habits and he slept soundly most nights without entering his dream world. Edward was growing fast and had started to stand unaided on his wobbly little legs but the wariness of his father returned to haunt Gabriel who consequently spent less and less time with his son. Naomi kept reassuring her husband that it was only a phase that Edward was going through and his dream of taking their son fishing one day was to be anticipated with pride. At work, only Joshua sensed any change in Gabriel's character and put his occasional 'walkabouts', as he called them, down to his son's way of coping with the loss of his sister.

Gabriel had not taken long to determine the approximate position where he had last seen Maggie. Though the view of the top of the beach had been vastly different from his present one, he was able to use the position of St Andrew's Church to gauge the spot to within a few yards. An opportunity on one particularly warm afternoon towards the end of September afforded him more time than usual to visit his favourite spot. Joshua had parish council business that afternoon and the *Richard Goodman* had returned at lunchtime from a brief morning fishing trip. Though the sun was warm and shining into his eyes, he was determined not to drift off to sleep. He wanted to be sure that any transmogrification happened while he was wide awake. St Andrew's Church clock chimed three times. Gabriel turned his head to look inland and suddenly she was there, trotting and skipping down the beach. It was Maggie, and she seemed happy as she approached him.

"Hello, Gabriel, I knew you'd be here."

The first thing Gabriel noticed was her clothes. They consisted of a dark purple uniform overlaid with a white but heavily stained tabard. He could just make out an emblem near the shoulder. It read, '*Castle Hill School*'. The sun had gone behind a cloud and Gabriel hardly noticed the panoramic view of Fenton had again moved forward in time; neither did he notice his own clothes, which had become those suitable for a sixteen-year-old boy.

"Hello, Maggie. It's nice to see you."

Maggie sat down beside Gabriel.

"I don't live at home anymore, Gabriel."

"Oh?"

"I live miles from here in a special place."

"How did you get here, then?"

"Oh, that's easy. I can go anywhere I want to now. I just have to think hard about it and, hey presto, I'm there."

"What's this special place?"

"Well, it's like a school for naughty children. I've been really bad, you know."

"Won't you be missed?"

"No, silly, I'm still there really."

"But …?"

"Like you, Gabriel, I'm a kind of ghost at the moment," said Maggie with a grin.

"Don't ghosts have to be dead?"

"No, of course not. You're not dead, are you?"

Gabriel didn't reply. He was having difficulty coping with Maggie's new concept. Maggie continued with her explanation.

"I have friends all over the place and if I want to see them I leave my body behind and off I go. I do it when I'm supposed to be having an afternoon nap so no one comes into my room and talks to me."

"What if they did?"

"I'd look as though I was dead and they'd probably panic, but I'd only be sleeping."

Gabriel was finding it strange that Maggie seemed to be able to talk and discuss her condition as though she was an adult.

"How old are you now, Maggie?"

"Well, they think I'm six, but I'm really much older."

Gabriel smiled. He knew what he had to ask.

"Where is Mary?"

"She's gone, silly."

"Gone where?"

"Just gone."

"Are you Mary?"

Maggie frowned and didn't immediately respond to what was obviously an awkward question for her. Her face blackened.

"No! No! No! Mary's gone away," she shouted and started to get to her feet.

"Please don't go, Maggie. I want to tell you something."

Maggie sat down.

"What?"

"First, let me ask you another question. What happened to your brother, Ed?"

"I told you before; you're Ed, only you said you call yourself Gabriel now."

"Well, Maggie, I had a sister and she went away like your brother did."

"So?"

"So her name was Mary."

"Oh."

"Yes, and I think you are her."

"Me?"

"Yes, my sister has somehow become you. Like Ed lives in my body, Mary lives in yours."

Maggie leapt to her feet and screamed,

"I hate you! I hate you! Mary has gone! I'm Maggie, I tell you, and you're stupid!"

Kicking sand behind her, she ran back up the beach, disappearing from Gabriel's view before she reached the promenade. The discussion had all been too much for her.

It took Gabriel a long time to recover his composure after such a strange encounter but he knew he had sorted several things out in his mind. After about half an hour of quiet contemplation, he got to his feet to make his way back to his home on the cliff top. He hadn't taken more than a couple of steps when his eyes finally took in the scene in front of him. He pinched his left forearm to check he wasn't dreaming. He was still in the future and probably 1985 if his memory served him right. He sat down again. Surely he would soon go back to his own time, like before when he'd come through the portal, only he hadn't come through the portal this time, had he? And then, for almost the first time, he looked down at himself. His physical appearance seemed to have changed again. He must be about sixteen, he decided, as Maggie had told him when they had met the previous time on the beach. How had he got back before? The he remembered shouting for help. He got to his feet and shouted as loud as he could,

"Help me – where am I? Oh, God, please help me get home!"

"What's up, lad. Are you lost?"

A dog barked at his ankles. The elderly man repeated his question.

"Are you lost, lad?"

"What? Oh, no, I'm fine, sir."

The man walked away, muttering something about the kids of today. Gabriel began to panic. His plea hadn't worked and he was still stuck in a time warp. All comfortable thoughts of his meeting with Mary/Maggie disappeared from his mind. He turned and ran up the beach. He had to try to find his home and Naomi and his son. He suddenly missed her terribly, caught, as he was, between his own reality and that of another age.

The first thing he noticed as he reached the stone promenade was the number of people about. It hadn't so far occurred to him that afternoon that it might not be the same time of year as when he had first wandered to his favourite spot from the South Quay about an hour earlier.

Though he tried to walk slowly and casually along the promenade, he soon began to draw some questioning stares from people passing by. In turn, he was torn between marvelling at their strange clothes and trying to find a way to his initial destination. He had to stop once or twice as he observed a couple of young girls about his age that were wearing some strange ear muffs clipped over their head, despite it clearly being a summer's day. When, as he passed them, he could hear some strange music coming from the muffs, he stopped and stared at them himself. His new world was a strange and wonderful place. Other sights and sounds took his breath away as he constantly gasped to himself, and when he saw a huge stone and iron type structure jutting at least a quarter of a mile out into the sea, he actually murmured out loud in utter surprise,

"Where is the North Quay and all the boats – they have disappeared!"

Fortunately, no one seemed to have heard him. He stopped walking and looked at the cliffs. The path he used to get to his house had disappeared, too, to be replaced by a series of zigzagging black-surfaced paths. He glanced back along the promenade and could just make out what he thought was the South Quay, though it now seemed to form one arm of a newly-built harbour with strange looking boats and pleasure craft, the like of which he'd never seen before. One other thing had gradually dawned on him on his short walk so far – it was around midday and probably a month or so earlier than his own time, judging by the height of the sun.

"You alright, son? Are you looking for something?"

"No, sir," replied Gabriel quickly. "Can you tell me the date, please?"

The middle-aged man grinned.

"The date – are you kidding me?"

"I don't know what that means, sir."

"Are you winding me up?"

Now Gabriel was totally confused as he tried to imagine how the man could be wound up like a clock.

"I just want to know what the date is, please."

"It's August the 26th, lad, and it's a Bank Holiday."

"Thank you, sir," replied Gabriel and he made a dash for the nearest of the black paths before the man could ask him anymore difficult questions. As he did so, he found himself thankful that he had recognised one thing, namely the name of a familiar public holiday, despite it having moved from the first Monday in August as he knew it. It gave him an explanation of the crowds on the promenade. At least they still had Bank Holidays, but 'winding people up' – that was a whole new game!

So, he thought, as he followed the maze of winding paths to the cliff top, it's the end of August. Nearing the top, he glanced wistfully southwards where South Beach Terrace ought to be but it didn't seem to him to still exist. There were no wooden cottages to be seen anywhere – only larger three-storeyed brick-built buildings that fronted another black-surfaced road like the one he had crossed at the foot of the cliffs. Soon, the path opened out onto another road and there, fifty yards to his left, he spotted Naomi's parents' house, *Fair View*. He was excited. It was the first familiar sight and maybe it could help him to return to his own time. Strange looking and brightly coloured horseless carriages lined one side of the road and two such vehicles flashed by him as he attempted to cross it. Once he had negotiated the road, he noticed that the building seemed taller with an extra storey on top. More mechanical noises droned in his ears. He was frightened. He wanted to hide from the fast moving monsters. There was a sign outside. He walked up to it and read the wooden board:

Fair View Guest House
All Rooms En-Suite
Children and Pets Welcome
No Vacancies

Gabriel studied the sign for a moment. *Fair View* was no longer a private dwelling and though he wasn't sure what the word '*en-suite*' meant, he guessed that Guest House was the same as Boarding House. Boldly, he walked up the path and pushed open the front door. He had to start somewhere. There was desk marked *Reception* and he approached the lady behind it. He tried to be as polite as he could be, hoping she would understand him.

"Good afternoon, Madam, I'm looking for the owner of this house."

The bespectacled woman glanced up from a book she appeared to be reading. She looked Gabriel up and down. She did not seem amused.

"Go away, you stupid boy. This is for residents only."

"But I live here, my lady."

"I'll give you *my lady,* indeed. Now get off the premises before I call the police."

"No, please don't – my name is Gabriel Thomas and I live here."

The lady reached for a black instrument on the desk in front of her. She held it to her ear and pressed some buttons below. Gabriel watched in awe, unable to move when, after a few seconds, she began to talking into the strange object.

"Hello, is that Sergeant Hughes? This is Daphne Lewis from *Fair View*."

There was a slight pause.

"Well, we have an intruder on the premises and he won't leave, I'm afraid."

Gabriel turned and ran. He just caught the woman's last words: "Quite tall and about sixteen or seventeen, I should say; scruffy black hair and old clothes – white shirt and brown corduroy trousers; probably a gypsy."

Once outside, he began to panic and felt trapped. This nightmare was far worse than any he had experienced in his dreams. Where could he go? He broke into a run and headed away from the cliffs. There was little that he recognised as he dashed down streets which hadn't existed in his time, dodging the mechanical monsters that continued to flash by him. Strange noises blared from them – a mixture of trumpet-like sounds and high-pitched screeches. Suddenly, another screech and a voice shouted from one of the vehicles.

"Get out of the road, you idiot! Get on the path!"

So that was it, you weren't allowed to run on the black bit. Gabriel ran to the side, almost knocking an elderly lady over. She screamed her anger.

"You stupid boy!"

Immediately ahead, he saw another, wider road with glass-fronted shops. He glanced up at the sign on the corner: *High Street*. He ran forward. Another screeching noise deafened him and he felt a sudden and sharp pain in his right side. Seconds before his mind went blank, he thought he could hear people shouting but their words never registered with him as an all-enveloping blackness descended on his world.

16
Two Scans

It was quite by chance that anyone looked in on Maggie that August Bank Holiday afternoon. There was only a skeleton staff on duty but they still outnumbered the permanent residents at Castle Hill. Many of the less problematic boarders had been allowed home for the weekend, leaving only Maggie and a couple of other of the more challenging 'patients', as a few of the residents were regarded. Senior Nurse, Jacky Wardlow, had drawn the short straw for the Monday shift and, at three o'clock, with little to occupy her time, she decided to make a quick tour of the resident's wing. After tapping gently on Maggie's door for a few seconds without response, she let herself in using her master key. Maggie appeared to be asleep which, at first sight, seemed quite normal to Jacky, given her charge's depressive state. On closer inspection of the little girl, however, she noticed that her eyes were wide open and staring at the ceiling.

"Are you alright, Maggie?"

Maggie's eyes did not flicker. Jacky Wardlow bent over and gently massaged her shoulder. She felt cold to the touch and she still did not respond. The nurse quickly picked up Maggie's wrist and felt for a pulse, breathing a sigh of relief when she detected one, even though it was faint and irregular. The six-year-old seemed to be in a coma. Nurse Wardlow fled for help and, being the senior nurse in charge, it meant a phone call to one of the consultants at the County Hospital, as well as an emergency call for an ambulance. It was five past three.

The ambulance arrived at twenty past, by which time, Dr Ableson had been alerted. He would meet his patient at the hospital. Jacky Wardlow accompanied Maggie in the ambulance for the ten minute drive across Hamsden. They had only gone a few hundred yards when Maggie suddenly let out a scream and ripped the oxygen mask from her face.

"I hate you! I hate you! Mary has gone! I'm Maggie, I tell you, and you're stupid!"

Frail though she had seemed, she leapt off the trolley, flinging her blanket to the floor. The paramedic gasped in horror and cursed himself for not securing her with straps as she made for the rear doors, with seemingly every intention of jumping out of the ambulance.

"Grab her, nurse!" he shouted, but Jacky Wardlow already had her in her arms.

"Get off me!" screamed Maggie. The paramedic reached for his bag and filled a syringe with sedative as quickly as he could.

"Hold her down, Nurse."

Though she fought like a wild thing, scratching, biting and kicking, the syringe found its spot in one of her buttocks and within a minute or so, her flailing limbs ceased moving. Nurse Wardlow laid her carefully on the trolley. The paramedic, bleeding from a scratch to his arm, secured the straps around her body. Jacky Wardlow was breathing heavily from several kicks to her abdomen but was otherwise unharmed. The paramedic quickly applied a dressing to his scratches just as the driver pulled the ambulance onto the casualty forecourt.

After Maggie was put into one of the casualty bays, Dr Ableson listened in silence as Jacky Wardlow and the paramedic gave their report. He sighed audibly when he learnt of the ferocity of Maggie's assault on them.

"You'd better get yourself checked over, nurse. Fits like that can give even a little girl superhuman strength."

Jacky Wardlow still seemed shaken and replied,

"I just don't understand it, Doctor. She was in a coma when I looked in on her and there was hardly any pulse and yet, within twenty minutes, she was like a demented harpy."

"She is a serious case, you know, and anything is possible with her."

"Well, I'm not going to go in her room again without assistance."

"You probably won't see her again at Castle Hill. I suspect I will be recommending a more secure unit."

"Canford?"

"We'll see, nurse. We'll have to do some more scans to see how the brain has deteriorated. I see from her notes that her next round of monthly tests was due tomorrow so she might as well stay here in our psychiatric unit tonight. I will alert the family this evening. In any case, I will see them tomorrow afternoon when they attend for Maggie's scan as usual. They weren't going to Castle Hill today, were they?"

"No, I don't think so," replied Jacky Wardlow.

In fact, Jenny and Gary had decided to spend the Bank Holiday with Gary's mother in Hamsden and they did not get back to Fenton till gone seven. Their visits to see their daughter had become less frequent with Maggie rarely showing any recognition. Jenny had returned to her job at *Curls and Twirls* and sometimes she took her lunch to Castle Hill to sit with her daughter for an hour. The phone rang at seven-thirty. Gary was in the shower and Jenny answered. Her heart missed a beat when she heard the familiar twang.

"Jenny, it's Sam Ableson. I rang earlier but you must have been out."

"Oh, hello, Doctor."

"Jenny, I'm afraid Maggie's taken a turn for the worse and we've had to transfer her to our unit at the hospital tonight. I don't want you to worry unduly but I didn't want you to go to Castle Hill expecting her to be there. You are coming for the tests tomorrow at two, aren't you?"

"Ye-es, I am but Gary can't make it."

"Oh, I think in the circumstances that he should try to be there."

Jenny went quiet.

"Are you still there, Jenny?"

"Yes, what is the problem?"

"I can't give you all the details over the phone. Suffice it to say that we have the situation under control but these tests are likely to be important."

"We'll both be there," said Jenny.

"Good – see you tomorrow, then. Goodbye."

"Bye."

Jenny replaced the phone in its cradle and sat down on the bottom stair. Gary peered over the banister rail.

"Who was that, Jen?"

Jenny did not look up. Gary could hear his wife's sobs. He was soon at her side.

"Whatever is the matter, love? Is it Maggie?"

"Yes, Dr Ableson says she's got worse but wouldn't tell me what had happened – just that the situation was under control, whatever that means. She's been transferred to the County Hospital psychiatric unit, he said. Oh, Gary, what's going to happen?" Jenny sobbed.

"I don't know, love – she has her tests tomorrow. You'll find out then."

"You've got to come with me, Gary – Dr Ableson says so."

"That will be tricky, Jen, I've got customers to see."

"Gary, you've just got to come. Nothing is more important than your daughter. Besides, we agreed we would do everything that Dr Ableson told us to do and, anyway, I want you to come with me."

"O.K., love, we'll go together. I suppose this is the next plateau."

"Yes, and God alone knows what that will mean," said Jenny as she buried her face in her husband's cotton bathrobe.

They were nearly ten minutes late the following day; a combination of a last minute customer for Gary and heavy traffic in the town centre. Maggie had already gone for her scan when they arrived at the psychiatric unit and they were met by Dr Abelson's assistant, Sally.

"Dr Ableson is with Maggie now," she said.

"Oh, I'm sorry we're late; the traffic was awful in town."

"That's alright; no problem. Will you wait here?"

"Yes," replied Jenny. "How is she? What happened yesterday?"

"She's reasonably quiet now; Dr Abelson will explain when he has the results of the scan."

"Has she said anything?"

"Not much, er, just …."

"Just what?" said Gary. "What did she say? Did she ask after us?"

"No, she just mentioned someone called Gabriel and got quite aggressive with one of the nurses when she told her that there was no one of that name here."

"Aggressive?" Jenny looked nervous and held Gary's hand.

"Yes, apparently she told the nurse that this Gabriel was here in the hospital and she had to go and see him. We've had to put the restraints on her because she kept trying to get out of bed. Poor Nurse Collins has a black eye from her flailing arms."

"Oh, I'm so sorry," said Jenny. "We didn't realise that she'd become that violent."

Sally smiled as if to say, *'you don't know the half of it'*.

"Dr Ableson will be able to tell you more later."

The psychiatrist's assistant was about to leave when she turned back and said,

"I don't suppose you know who this Gabriel is, do you?"

"Oh," replied Jenny, "it's just the name she has for her make-believe friend. She used to have a doll she called Mary and we didn't know where she got that name either."

Less than twenty-four hours earlier, Gabriel could hear things but he couldn't see.

'So, what is the extent of his injuries?'

'Well the most worrying is the fractured skull, just above his right eye but, in addition, he has a few broken ribs; his right shoulder is dislocated and his wrist is broken. Apart from some severe bruising, he had been lucky to survive the accident, I'm told. The car was doing more than forty down the High Street in Fenton. The driver has been arrested.'

'I see, and do we know who this young man is yet?'

'No one has a clue; even the local police aren't acquainted with him, given he looked like a gypsy; his clothes were old and from another age. He wouldn't have looked out of place at a Victorian fairground or something similar. They've put out a request for information on the radio for anyone to come forward who might know him.'

'Wasn't he carrying any form of identification?'

'Well, that's the strange thing, you know; all he had on him was some coins and a pocket knife with the initials GT engraved on the side.

As for identification, you know what these gypsies are like. Sometimes even their own parents don't know how many children they have.'

'How much money was he carrying?'

'Very little, but it what was what the coins were that was odd. They were all Victorian and dated between 1885 and 1895'.

'Hm, just some old coins, eh?'

'No, and that's just the point; they weren't old.'

'I thought you said they were Victorian.'

'I did but they looked brand new – shiny copper and silver, including florins and farthings, which have been out of circulation for ages. If I hadn't seen them with my own eyes, Richard, when I took charge of him down in casualty, I wouldn't have believed it.'

'What about the knife; any clues there?'

'Only if there's someone missing whose initials are GT and, so far, no one's come forward. It's a complete mystery'.

'Well, I suppose it's not our job to worry about who he is. We've got to repair him as best we can and, to be honest, looking at his skull fracture I would be extremely surprised if his brain ever functions properly again. If no one comes to claim him, we may never know who he is and he'll have to go into an institution of some kind, depending on his mental abilities after his physical injuries heal. I suspect it will be a mental hospital.'

'That would be such a shame for such a young man, who despite his injuries is clearly a handsome brute. I've never seen such jet-black hair before.'

'Right, thank you for standing in for me down in casualty; his scan results should be back within the hour. You can check with me later, if you're interested.'

'Oh, I will, Richard, and I am *interested. It's a curious case.'*

The scan, when it came, confirmed most of Dr Richard Sutton's prognosis of the unknown boy's condition. The front right side of the brain had suffered severe trauma and the patient's cognitive abilities would be badly affected, he concluded. Though he might learn to make a few sounds in time, the likelihood was that he would be totally blind and suffer severe mental problems.

This time, Jenny and Gary had to wait for nearly two hours for Dr Ableson to return with Maggie's scan results. Jenny took one look at his face and she knew the news was bad. Sam Ableson sat both parents down and began by relating the shocking events of the day before. He concluded by saying,

"So, she has become violent, I'm afraid."

"What about the scan, Doctor?" said Gary.

"It confirms what I expected – her mental condition has deteriorated quickly. And beyond what Castle Hill are able to cope with."

Jenny was forthright as she tried to hide her emotions.

"So, she's gone mad?"

The psychiatrist did not answer but just smiled sympathetically. It was how his profession always broke such news. Jenny did not cry. Gary hung is head. It was over; the news could not get worse and that provided some comfort to Maggie's parents. Neither of them heard much of what Dr Ableson then said as he explained the provision for Maggie's future care. The recently refurbished old asylum and former workhouse near Canford was to be their daughter's home for the rest of her life.

17

The Black-Haired Gypsy Boy

Time would hold little relevance for Gabriel over the next few weeks. The doctors continued to assess his condition daily, hoping for the miracle they doubted would ever come. No one had come forward to claim or identify the strange patient and the mystery surrounding him remained unsolved. The one person who had heard the name of the strange boy, Daphne Lewis, owner of the *Fair View* guest house, had shut her establishment immediately after the Bank Holiday weekend and had returned to London with her husband till the end of November when they would return for the Christmas season. Sergeant Owen Hughes had taken several statements from people who had seen or even spoken to the black-haired gypsy boy but they all said more or less the same thing: He didn't seem to have all his marbles.

Despite predictions, towards the end of September, some encouraging signs were noted in his condition. Partial sight seemed to have been restored as well as some movement to his limbs. His eyes seem to follow the doctors and nurses as they tended to his needs, and occasionally, he would raise an arm in acknowledgement at their presence at his bedside. However his eyes remained staring and with a wild look in them, Dr Sutton would remain convinced of his likely unstable mental condition. All his physical injuries had healed, surprising the doctors with the speed of the process.

Gabriel heard many sounds over those weeks, most of which he did not understand, but one voice kept coming back to him and he was never sure if the person speaking was at his bedside or if the familiar tones were just inside his head. The words were more or less always the same but on the first Friday in October, the voice became more insistent. Gabriel was awake and his body seemed more alive than normal. He could feel sensations he hadn't felt for some time. He had no memory of his accident with the 'mechanical monster' and the feeling that he should be elsewhere had only just returned. He knew he just didn't belong with these people who seemed to talk a foreign language about things of which he had no knowledge. He didn't want to be there and the only comfort was his sister's voice, or did it belong to Maggie, her reincarnation? Mary's voice that afternoon seemed to play on these new feelings.

'You've got to come and join me, Gabriel; it's nice here.'

Gabriel's lips tried to form the obvious question, but no sound came forth. Mary seemed to understand his difficulty.

'It's alright, Gabriel, I will show you. You've just got to get out of that place. I was there once but they brought me here. We go on walks and pick flowers. You'll like it when you come.'

Gabriel felt warm inside. Mary/Maggie continued.

'Just run away and be quick before someone comes. You'll know which way to go and I'll be waiting for you. You've got to show them that you belong here. They'll know when you come.'

"I'm coming, Maggie."

The black-haired gypsy boy had spoken his first words in six weeks but there had been no one there to hear them. He screwed up his face in concentration. What was left of his mind reacted quickly and the bedcovers were thrown back as Gabriel flung himself onto the floor. No one had seen the need to put restraints on him. He crouched like an animal and listened, but no one came. He scrambled to the half-open window; his mind unable to process the purpose of the door behind him. The sky outside seemed to provide him with hope. He pushed on the window with all his strength and hurled himself through the opening. Fortunately, his room was on the ground floor and he fell just a few feet onto the soft wet grass below. It had been pouring with rain and his pyjamas would provide little protection from the cold. His sight was not good but it was sufficient to make out the open space of the adjoining car park. He ran, ape-like, for it. The further he went the more upright he became so that, by the time he had reached the main gates, he was running almost like a normal human being. He could hear voices shouting behind him. He dived for cover, provided by a small copse of trees and bushes across the road. He knew he had to hide. Some people were chasing him. They didn't want him to go. He crouched low to the ground and waited.

'Just close your eyes, Gabriel.'

Mary was close. Gabriel did as he was told.

"Now open them."

There were trees all around him; the woods seemed familiar. Maggie was beside him. A short distance away, a woman was staring straight at him. She had a startled expression on her face.

"Who are you, young man, and what are you doing here in those wet pyjamas? Where on earth did you spring from?"

"He's mad, like me," said Maggie.

"Well, where have you come from?"

The speaker was wearing a blue uniform.

"He's come home," continued Maggie.

"Oh, be quiet, Maggie, and let him speak."

"But he's come to see me."

"Well, young man?"

"I've come home to Mary."

"Who's Mary?"

The staff at the County Hospital would find no trace of the black-haired gypsy boy near the hospital that day and the police were quickly informed of his escape. The public were warned not to approach him as he was likely to be violent and unpredictable, they said. The warder, who took him back to Canford Mental Hospital that afternoon, failed to give the authorities an accurate time when she had found the wandering vagrant in Canford woods. It had been a treat for Maggie to be allowed a stroll among the richly tinted trees, clothed in their autumn glory. Police and hospital staff would puzzle for days over how the pyjama-clad gypsy boy could have made the seven mile journey, unaided, from the hospital to Canford without being seen, especially when his bare feet seemed barely marked. If accurate timings had been kept, they would have realised that the journey just couldn't have taken place in the allotted time.

Gabriel was kept in the former Victorian asylum that night and his residency was soon to become permanent when, after several tests, both by its own doctors and Drs Sutton and Ableson, it was concluded that he was a serious risk to himself and society. After one week, he was judged to be mentally insane. He was given the name Gabriel after little Maggie had christened him that on the way back from her stroll in the woods.

18

A Walk in the Woods

He was happy, happier than he'd been in a long time. He didn't dream anymore. His new reality was simple and his damaged brain had little to tax it. He had no memory of his previous life as a fisherman in Victorian England. He was a child again and he had a new sister to play with whenever he wanted. She was now younger than him and seemed as sane as he was or, at least, their mental abilities were in harmony. They enjoyed simple things and felt no fear, wanted for nothing and were rid of most evil aspects of human life. A butterfly was just a butterfly and flowers were to be picked and smelt. Trees provided shade and nests for birds – not wood for man's uses. They played games outside in the grounds; games that only they knew; games they never tired of. Occasionally, they were taken for walks, visiting the neighbouring woods, but never as far as the eastern edge which still brought frightening memories back to Gabriel.

It was a beautiful spring day and the trees had started to bud. Their custodian had let them walk a few yards ahead. They started to talk.

"Why are you called Gabriel?"

"Why are you called Maggie?"

"I don't know."

"Where do you live?"

"I don't know."

"Did you die, Mary?"

"I don't know. Did you, Ed?"

"I'm not Ed."

"I'm not Mary; she went away."

"Where did she go?"

"I don't know."

"Will she come back?"

"I don't know."

"Do you like me?"

"Yes. Do you like me?"

"Yes."

They stopped talking; it had been a simple, naïve conversation, if judged by normal standards. For Maggie and Gabriel, it had been their way of reassuring themselves of their identities; they felt safe and would be with each other forever, living or dead. They would walk the woods together and, one day, they would go through the portal together, a brother and sister, never to be parted.

THE END

Gabriel's Dreams
Martyn Croft
Copyright © 2009 Martyn Croft
Cover Image by Digital Vision / Getty Images
Cover Image by Digital Vision / Getty Images

www.ingramcontent.com/pod-product-compliance
Ingram Content Group UK Ltd.
Pitfield, Milton Keynes, MK11 3LW, UK
UKHW041437180426
11947UKWH00007B/498